THE FRIENDSHIP WAR

FAVORITES BY ANDREW CLEMENTS

About Average
Extra Credit
Frindle
The Jacket
The Landry News
The Last Holiday Concert
The Losers Club
Lost and Found
Lunch Money
The Map Trap
No Talking
The Report Card
The School Story
Troublemaker
A Week in the Woods

and many others!

THE FRIENDSHIP WAR

ANDREW CLEMENTS

RANDOM HOUSE NEW YORK

Text copyright © 2019 by Andrew Clements
Jacket art and interior illustrations copyright © 2019 by Laura Park

All rights reserved. Published in the United States by Random House Children's Books, a division of Penguin Random House LLC, New York.

Random House and the colophon are registered trademarks of Penguin Random House LLC.

Visit us on the Web! rhcbooks.com

Educators and librarians, for a variety of teaching tools, visit us at RHTeachersLibrarians.com

Library of Congress Cataloging-in-Publication Data
Name: Clements, Andrew, author.
Title: The friendship war / Andrew Clements.
Description: First edition. | New York : Random House, [2019] | Summary: When Grace takes boxes of old buttons from a building her grandfather bought, she starts a fad at school that draws her closer to one friend, but further from another.
Identifiers: LCCN 2017034192 | ISBN 978-0-399-55759-0 (hardcover) | ISBN 978-0-399-55760-6 (hardcover library binding) | ISBN 978-0-399-55761-3 (ebook)
Subjects: | CYAC: Best friends—Fiction. | Friendship—Fiction. | Buttons—Collectors and collecting—Fiction. | Fads—Fiction. | Schools—Fiction.
Classification: LCC PZ7.C59118 Fp 2019 | DDC [Fic]—dc23

Printed in the United States of America
10 9 8 7 6 5 4 3 2 1
First Edition

For
Audrey L. Werner,
a dear friend
and an inspiration to countless teachers,
including me

1

All of Them

Flying from Chicago to Boston by myself hasn't been as big a deal as my dad said it was going to be. But nothing ever is. The second I turn on my phone, it dings with three texts from him:

Dad

12:46

> Text me as soon as you land.

12:48

> Your plane should have landed by now.

12:50

> Are you all right?

So I text him right away:

> All good, just landed. Love from Boston!

Dad worries. He calls it planning, but it's worry.

Mom worries less because she knows I don't do dumb stuff—not on purpose. My brother, Ben, knows that, too. Actually, Ben understands me pretty well. I understand him totally, which isn't that hard. He's fifteen, and he mostly thinks about two things: girls and music.

Ben's music isn't rock or jazz or rap. It's marching band. Which makes his girlfriend-hunt tougher than it needs to be. At least, that's my theory. It's the whole marching-with-a-clarinet-while-wearing-a-cowboy-hat thing. However, if it hadn't been for Ben's August band camp, the entire family might be here on the plane with me, and I wouldn't be getting to spend time alone with Grampa.

So, hooray for marching band!

And if Dad had been a little less worried, then he and Mom probably wouldn't have gotten me my own iPhone a couple of weeks ago.

So, hooray for dads who worry!

Grampa's waiting right at the end of the walkway from the plane, just like Dad told him to.

"Hey, Grace! Welcome to Boston!"

"Hi, Grampa! You look great!"

I'm not saying that to be polite or something.

When we all came to Massachusetts last summer, it was for Gramma's funeral, and back then Grampa seemed way too thin. And old.

He looks much better now, and when we hug, I can tell he's not so skinny anymore.

The flight attendant in charge of me looks at Grampa's driver's license. After he signs a form, we're on the move, me with my backpack and him pulling my suitcase.

"Anything at baggage claim?"

"Nope."

"Good. So we're headed for Central Parking . . . unless you're hungry."

"Dad loaded me up with tons of food. I could survive on the leftovers for weeks."

"That's my son-in-law the Eagle Scout—'Once an Eagle, always an Eagle!'" Then he says, "Hey, did you see that link I sent you about how they're making jet fuel out of vegetable oil?"

"Yeah, I loved that!"

Of all the people in the world, I think Grampa understands me best. He's a real estate agent, but he likes math and science almost as much as I do. Last week we swapped texts while we watched an episode of *Nova*, and for years he's been emailing me links to news he finds online—like the article about robots that can travel through space, and they can keep building new copies of themselves, and they do that for *thousands* of years until the whole galaxy gets explored!

Except . . . I can't prove that Grampa is really into the science stuff. He might be making himself like it because he knows that *I* like it.

Either way, it's pretty great.

At the car, Grampa loads my gear into the trunk.

"How about you lean back and take a nap. When we get to Burnham, I'll wake you up for some ice cream. And I've got a surprise for you, too."

"A surprise? What?"

"Not telling."

"Well . . . can the surprise come first, before the ice cream?"

That gets a chuckle. "Excellent idea."

It's so good to hear Grampa laugh!

We get going, but I don't want to sleep. I want to stay awake and talk.

Especially about Gramma.

Except it might be too soon for him to talk about her. It's still kind of soon for me, too. During third and fourth grades I called her a couple of times every week, and she just let me talk and talk. I could call her about anything, or about nothing. And if I ran out of stuff to say, she always had something new to tell me, especially about her garden and all the plants and insects and animals. If Gramma hadn't been so great at describing every little thing she loved, no way would I have gotten into science like I have.

Anyway, I know we both miss her. Which must be a lot different for Grampa than it is for me. He knew her for so much longer. Compared to him, maybe I hardly knew her at all.

It'd be nice to talk, but I got up at five-thirty this morning and I stayed awake to watch a movie on the plane. Once we reach the highway, the humming tires wipe me out.

"Where are we?"

I blink and look around, and I remember.

The road into Burnham is up near the New Hampshire border, and it winds through hills covered with pine and maple trees. We pass old farmhouses, most of them white, with green or black shutters. There are two apple orchards, then corn and pumpkin fields surrounded by stone walls. Land in Illinois doesn't look like this.

The air feels different, too—less humid, sort of crisp, even in the last week of August. Grampa explained once how the soil here is so rocky that it can't hold moisture the way it does in Illinois—and that got us started on learning about the North American glaciers during the last Ice Age.

We get to the town center, and Grampa says, "Shut your eyes, and don't peek till I say."

So I close my eyes.

And then I pretend I've been kidnapped and blindfolded—which is probably a weird thing to do. But it makes my observations seem like they matter.

I feel the car go straight, and I slow-count to thirty before we stop. Maybe a traffic light? No . . . a stop sign, because we move ahead, then stop, move ahead, stop. And the turn signal is clicking.

Okay . . . so we went thirty seconds at about thirty miles an hour. I do the math, and since going sixty miles per hour means traveling one mile per minute, going *thirty* miles per hour means going *half* a mile per minute. And we just traveled half a minute, so we went about one-quarter of a mile.

Which is what I'll tell the police when I call them with the phone that I cleverly hid in my left sock. So they can figure out how to track the kidnappers. And rescue me.

The car turns left, and I count up to a hundred and fifteen before we slow to a stop, and I hear the turn signal again. So, almost two minutes at thirty miles per hour, which is one mile.

Then it's a sharp right, some bumps and squeaks, and a full stop.

"Okay—open your eyes now!"

I'm looking at a gravel parking lot full of tall weeds, and we're next to a long brick building. Up near the roof there's a painted sign with faded letters: BURNHAM MILLS.

"I bought this whole place just last week! Isn't it great?"

Grampa sounds like Ben after he got his new clarinet.

"Yeah, it's *great*!" And there's a lot of zip in my voice because I can tell he wants me to love it.

But as I'm snapping pictures with my phone, all I'm seeing is a good spot to make a zombie movie—or hide a kidnapped girl.

The windows on the ground floor of the building are boarded up, the second- and third-floor windows are mostly broken, and the brick walls are covered with graffiti. Cracked granite steps lead up to gray metal doors held shut by a rusted chain and a padlock.

"I *love* this place! It cost me almost nothing, and by next year, the first floor'll be full of nice little shops, with beautiful offices and river-view condos up above. Before you go home, I'm going to give you the grand tour. But let's head back to Main Street and get that ice cream."

It's funny, but I can't remember Grampa ever doing something like this before—I thought that he just helped *other* people buy and sell properties. And part of me wonders if he'd be tackling a project like this if Gramma were here.

I tell myself that this is scientific curiosity, but I know I'm just being nosy.

A day at the ocean, a day climbing Mount Monadnock, a morning hike around Boston, and an afternoon at the Museum of Science.

Grampa is definitely back, and that makes me really happy. We've been walking so much that I'm feeling like I'll need a vacation from my vacation.

The day before I fly home, we're on the front steps of Grampa's old building late in the afternoon. He really wants to take me inside the place.

"Here—put this on."

And he hands me an orange hard hat with a headlamp.

"It's *dark* in there?"

Scientifically, I understand that darkness isn't an actual condition. Light is actual, and darkness just means no light. Still, I'm not a fan.

"It's not dark everywhere—only where the windows are boarded up. And in the stairwells. And down in the basement."

He has about ten different keys on a string, and he's trying to find the one for the padlock on the door.

"The mill was built in 1849, and along the back side? That's the Kepshaw River. The water turned a huge paddle wheel to make the power. First it was a carpet mill, then a woolen blanket mill, a cotton mill, a shoe factory, and finally a men's and women's clothing factory, which went out of business in 1946. After that, a printer and some small businesses and artists rented space, but it's been empty for almost fifteen years—which is why it was so cheap!"

I'm thinking it would be fine if we just look around the *outside* of the building, but Grampa gets the lock open and then hands me a canvas shopping bag.

"What's this for?"

"In case you find something interesting. You can keep whatever you like."

"Really? Anything?"

"Yup—I own the building and everything in it."

I follow him inside, and I'm using my phone, sometimes as an extra flashlight, sometimes as a camera. Right away, I realize that this treasure hunt is why Grampa wanted me to take the grand tour—he knows I love finding stuff, and the old mill is like a gold mine.

The first thing I discover is a solid brass doorknob, just

lying on the floor inside the mill office. Then I find two wooden bobbins loaded with red and green yarn, then a giant pair of scissors, a tin box of sewing needles, an iron gear that weighs about five pounds, two old-fashioned fountain pens, a silver thimble, a key ring with nine brass keys, a hammer with a big flat head, and a pair of antique glasses—the kind that pinch onto the nose. After an hour I feel like I've barely started. But we've got a dinner reservation at Grampa's favorite seafood place, so I'm trying to see the whole building before time runs out.

It's after five o'clock, and we're up on the third floor and it's bright and sunny, with sparrows and pigeons flying in and out the broken windows. There's not much to see: about twenty large wooden tables bolted to the floor, and some rusty sewing machines next to the windows. I'm watching where I step—bird droppings.

I point at a doorway on the far wall. "Where does that go?"

"Let's look."

It's locked, so Grampa gets out his keys, and it takes five tries to find the right one.

I turn on my headlamp and pull the door open. It's a small storage room—wooden shelves loaded with cardboard boxes, each one about a foot high and a foot wide. I brush off some dust and spiderwebs and carry a box out into the daylight of the large room. It's heavy. The paper sealing tape tears away easily, and inside . . . buttons. Plain dark gray buttons, each a little smaller than a dime.

I shove my hand deep into the box, grab some, and pull them up to look: just like the ones on top.

I bring out another box and open it, and then a third—nothing but more of the same.

Grampa says, "That's a *lot* of gray buttons—must be almost thirty boxes!"

"And it's okay if I take some of these, right?"

"Like I said, you can keep whatever you want."

I scoop two quick handfuls into my bag, then stop.

"But, really, Grampa, I'd like to have all of them."

He points at the shelves. "*All* of them?"

"Yes, please."

"What in the world are you going to do with that many buttons?"

"I don't know, but I still want them. If it's okay."

Now he's laughing.

"Sure, why not? Take 'em all!"

Then he looks over the shelves again, thinking.

"It might be a week or so before I can get them shipped, but the boxes should fit onto one pallet. And since you are my one and only granddaughter, I will make it happen! I just wish I could be there to see the look on your mom's face when the load arrives in Illinois!"

Latching onto these buttons? It's not weird, not for me. And Grampa knows that. And he knows Mom will understand, too. After all, she's the one who stops the car whenever I spot a garage sale. And Gramma? She would have clapped her hands and said, *Perfect!*

Grampa has seen my room at home, and how the drawers of my desk are crammed full. Also the top of my dresser, and the tops of my bookcases, and the windowsills—actually, every flat surface in my room is loaded, including the floor. Feathers, acorns, a really old calculator, seashells, troll dolls, fake jewelry, rocks and stones, keys, markers and pens, coins, pinecones, paper clips, candles from my birthday cakes, every card and letter I've ever gotten, old movie tickets, marbles, nails—on and on. And that's just the smaller stuff.

I've also got seven large snow globes, nine dark blue glass bottles, a globe of the world from 1941, a slide rule in its own leather case, three plastic crates of vinyl records, a wobbly piano stool, and a couple dozen stuffed animal toys—mostly cats and dogs and penguins. Not to mention half a zillion paperbacks and comic books. Plus three full sets of *Encyclopaedia Britannica*—which I stacked up into the shape of a big armchair.

I have a theory about why I collect so many things. Which I don't want to think about now.

Actually, I've usually got at least five or six active theories rolling around inside my head—theories about all kinds of stuff. Because whenever I notice something I don't understand, I think up a possible way to explain it, and then I keep track of the facts to test if my theory is right—which is not some new process I invented. It's called the scientific method.

Still, wanting to own a whole storeroom of buttons?

I might need to revise my theory about why I love all the things in my room.

But I'm not lying to Grampa—I really don't know why I want all of them. I just do. It feels like an opportunity I shouldn't pass up, like when I found that third set of *Encyclopaedia Britannica*.

And Grampa gets that. He's still chuckling and shaking his head.

I look him in the face. "Can I ask a favor?"

He wipes his eyes with a tissue. "Sure."

"When I get home and I tell Mom and Dad and Ben about your building and everything, I'm not going to tell them about the buttons, not till they arrive. So could you not mention them until later?"

"No problem—that's even better!"

He's laughing again.

Grampa probably thinks I'm going to keep these buttons a complete secret until they show up in Illinois. But that's not quite true.

I'm going to tell one other person in exactly six days— on the first day of school.

2

The Ellie Effect

It's strange not seeing Ellie all summer. For two and a half months we don't even email or talk on the phone. But I'm used to it. Her family has a vacation home in Colorado, and they also travel a lot—like, all over the world.

Sometimes I wonder if Ellie has an extra best friend in Aspen, like a spare tire. And sometimes I think that by the time we make it to June every year, we might just really *need* our long summer away from each other. With zero communication.

But today it's the first day of school, and I see her in the hall outside the art room. Then she turns her head, and we snap together like magnets for a quick hug.

I jump right in, because with Ellie, it's important to be the one who starts talking first.

"I've *got* to tell you something! At the end of August? I flew to Boston by myself to visit my grandfather, and he bought this really old building, and I—"

She grabs my arm. "That reminds me!"

And just like that, I know that my turn to talk is over.

"Because, in Aspen? Inside this Old West general store, there's a jewelry shop, and they make things out of real gold nuggets—that's all they do! Look at this bracelet. Isn't it *fantastic*? My mom would *die* if she knew I wore it today, but I *had* to show you! And these sneakers? You'll never guess where I got them—in *Paris*! My grandmother took me and my sister to all her favorite shops there, and it was wonderful! Such *gorgeous* things—you *have* to come for a sleepover! And on the way back to Colorado, we stayed in London for six days, and we went to this *amazing* store called Harrods, and I got the *cutest* . . ."

Ellie goes on for three more minutes, and her descriptions are funny and smart and charming and captivating—in other words, classic Ellie. But by the time she stops, I realize that I don't want to tell her about my *fantastic* dusty boxes of buttons, from this *gorgeous* crumbling building where all the floors were covered with the *cutest* bird droppings.

And this is when I remember the Ellie Effect. Every summer I forget about this phenomenon, which always makes me ask myself the same question: *If Ellie Emerson is my best friend, then how come she gets me so upset?*

I've been trying to figure this out since second grade, and there does not appear to be a scientific explanation.

So each new school year, I get to study the Ellie Effect all over again.

One time Mom said, *There's an old saying: "Oppo-*

sites attract." I think that might be what's going on with you and Ellie. In a lot of ways, this theory makes sense to me.

I don't care much about clothes; Ellie cares a lot.

I love math and science; Ellie doesn't.

I like to hike and camp and mess around outside; Ellie is perfectly happy to stay inside and talk . . . or go shopping. And honestly? Sometimes Ellie can be so much fun to be with that she can make *me* happy to hang out at the mall all day, too. Once in a while.

And those sneakers she got in Paris? I have to admit that they're really cute.

The one way that we seem *most* alike? We're both pretty—except I don't try to be, and Ellie does.

If I ever said that out loud—that I thought I was pretty? Everyone would think I was totally conceited. But I'm not. I'm just trying to be scientific about something science can't even define. There have to be a million different ideas about what makes someone good-looking. All I know for sure is this: Ellie is *positive* that she's pretty, and she keeps on telling me that I am, too.

But I hate the idea that if she *didn't* think I was pretty, then Ellie wouldn't like me as much. It's one theory I don't want to prove.

The warning bell rings, and as we walk into homeroom, I remind myself for the hundredth time that even though Ellie Emerson is my best friend, Ellie's opinions do *not* rule the world.

It only feels that way.

3

Smooshed

The next two days are super busy—all the regular beginning-of-school stuff, plus dealing with three new teachers, plus being swamped with homework, plus getting used to changing classes, which we didn't do last year.

Ellie's in my homeroom, in all my classes except for science and math, and we sit together at lunch, so we're seeing a lot of each other.

But I don't tell her about my trip to visit Grampa. Or about the stuff I found. Especially the buttons.

And I tell myself I don't care that for the past two years we've only had sleepovers at *her* house, never at mine.

Never.

And I keep telling myself I don't care what Ellie thinks about anything.

But I know that's not true. I know I'm ignoring scientific evidence.

How do I know this?

Because it's Thursday afternoon, and when I get off

the school bus, what do I see in our driveway? A wooden pallet, squat and square, loaded with twenty-seven cardboard boxes full of buttons.

And am I happy? Am I excited?

No. I feel like a total dork.

Right now I would gladly trade all these buttons for one pair of cute purple-and-orange sneakers.

From Paris.

There's a note from Mom inside the kitchen door—she's at Staples. And Ben won't get home till after his band practice.

So I find a pair of scissors, and I go back outside and snip the plastic wrapping off the pallet. I haul every box upstairs to my room, and then I drag the empty pallet to the side of the garage and lean it up next to the recycling barrels.

I feel hot and tired and grimy.

And stupid.

Back at the mill with Grampa? Owning all these buttons had seemed like such a wonderful idea. And now?

Not so much.

I have an old, wide brass bed with a dust ruffle, and twenty-four of the boxes fit underneath.

I stack the last three at the back of my closet, and now all the boxes are tucked away, but not really hidden.

So, of course, at bedtime, Mom notices.

"They're full of *what*?"

"Buttons, little gray buttons. Grampa and I found them in his old building, and he said I could have them."

"Well. That was very nice of him."

If Mom's upset, she doesn't show it.

And I have a theory about why:

When I was eight, I tried to collect all the acorns from the three big oak trees in our backyard. I filled bucket after bucket, and lugged each load up to my room to dump into a big blue plastic bin. When the storage bin was full, there were still tons of acorns left outside. Mom helped me estimate the number of acorns in my bin—more than eleven thousand! Then we searched online and discovered that in some years, one large oak tree can drop up to ten thousand acorns—which meant that there could have been almost *twenty thousand acorns* still lying outside on the ground! We also read how deer and crows and wild turkeys and chipmunks and blue jays and squirrels love to eat acorns. Learning all these facts stopped my gathering. But my big bin of acorns sat in a corner for almost a year—until the whole upstairs of our house began to smell like moldy leaves. Then the acorns went away.

So, these buttons? Mom probably thinks they won't stick around forever.

The first full week of sixth grade zipped by, and I've had no trouble ignoring the buttons—except I stubbed my big toe on a box as I climbed into bed. Twice.

Then halfway through Monday morning of week two, Mrs. Casey says, "We start our first social studies unit today: the Industrial Revolution in America." And on the whiteboard at the front of the room, she flashes a black-and-white illustration with a caption below it:

BOOTT COTTON MILLS • LOWELL, MASSACHUSETTS • 1852

Some of the buildings are long and low, and automatically, my hand flies up.

"Yes, Grace?"

"I went inside an old mill building in Massachusetts this summer. I took pictures, and I got to keep some things I found."

"Great! Could you share some of that with the class tomorrow?"

Actually . . . I would hate that.

This is what I want to say. But, of course, I can't.

So I say, "Sure."

"Good—thank you!"

Mrs. Casey turns back to the whiteboard. "Now, this picture shows a very large mill located beside the Merrimack River. In your reading at home tonight, I'd like you to find . . ."

I stop listening. My face feels warm, and I want to rewind the last minute and then delete it.

Because my things from the mill? They're part of that afternoon I spent with Grampa, poking around like archaeologists.

It was great telling Mom and Dad and Ben about the

mill and the things we found. They know how much I love flea markets and garage sales and old, run-down antiques shops.

Also, they understand about all the stuff in my bedroom. Some kids like to keep diaries and journals and online scrapbooks and selfies. Me? I like to keep *things*. And my room? It's like a museum of my life so far—that's my theory about all my stuff.

And I've got evidence to support this theory.

The smooth gray stone next to the lamp on my dresser? It makes me remember the morning mist above the lake on our first family camping trip to Wisconsin. The small curved twig next to the stone? I picked that up on the playground when I was in kindergarten because it looked like a smile. And that IBC Root Beer bottle cap? I had never drunk soda from a glass bottle until my first sleepover at Ellie's house.

Almost everything in my room is there because it links up with a particular moment, and those moments are mine.

And they're private.

But there's no way to stop this. Tomorrow, my happy memories of the mill are going to get squished and smooshed around until they turn into a social studies lesson.

I know *smooshed* is not a proper scientific term. But it's still the right word: *smooshed*.

The one good thing? As far as the other kids and

Mrs. Casey are concerned, my things from the mill will just look like a bunch of random historical objects.

Still, I hate that my summer souvenirs are going to be studied and examined by the whole class. And probably judged, too.

Especially by Ellie.

4

Discoveries

We're walking into the cafeteria Monday after social studies, and Ellie says, "How come you didn't tell me about your trip to Massachusetts? Did you go to see your grandfather? I remember you went for your grandmother's funeral last summer, right?"

Because I still haven't told Ellie anything about my trip. I had started to, back on the first day of school. But she doesn't remember that.

Before I can answer, Taylor comes up to us, and then lunch happens, and Ellie doesn't mention my trip again the whole rest of the day.

Which makes me wonder, *Does she actually want to know?*

Or actually care?

Maybe the question Ellie meant to ask me is, *Who else did you tell about your trip?* Because Ellie hates being left out.

News flash: Everyone hates that.

It's almost bedtime, and I send six images from my phone to Mrs. Casey's school email address.

Choosing the pictures to share up on the whiteboard tomorrow was easy: the mill building and the river behind it; the huge gears and driveshafts in the basement; views of the mill's office, with all the cubbyholes and built-in desks; and then some pictures of the large open spaces where the women and men worked at their machines or tables.

But there aren't any pictures of Grampa or me at the mill.

Those are private.

I load the things I found back into the same canvas shopping bag Grampa gave me—except for the buttons.

I had scooped some into my bag when we were at the mill, and now those are in a blue glass jar on my dresser—to remind me how I found them. With Grampa. Because those buttons are different from the ones that arrived on the pallet. And they're not for sharing.

I'm not sure I should take any buttons at all. I'd have to drag out a box, and then put it away again. . . . It'd be a lot of messing around just to show the class some buttons.

Down in the kitchen, I'm halfway through a cup of yogurt when I decide that buttons are part of the story, part of the mill's last chapter as a clothing factory. And really, all I have to do is open the top box on the stack in my closet.

So I take a plastic sandwich bag upstairs. I open my closet, shove some clothes aside, tear the tape off the box, pull back the flaps, and drop a handful of small gray buttons into the bag.

Except the buttons aren't gray or small—they're bright yellow, and almost an inch across!

And a theory jumps into my mind: At the mill, the buttons must have been organized by color, and the three boxes I opened were all from the *gray* section!

It takes me thirty minutes to move, open, and label each box of buttons. And my theory is correct: Not only do I own small gray ones, but I also have buttons that are red, green, pink, lavender, yellow, black, brown, amber, blue, and white—all different sizes, too, from bigger than a quarter to smaller than a pea.

And my favorite discovery? Three of the boxes are filled with all the leftover and mismatched and fancy buttons, so many different kinds! There are buttons made of glass, shell, brass, wood, plastic, pewter, leather, and other materials I don't recognize. I've got buttons that look like diamonds and pearls and roses and daisies; buttons in the shape of hearts and triangles and squares and stars and dogs and horses and cats and butterflies and snowflakes—on and on and on!

I want to dump all three of the mixed boxes onto my floor and then sort the buttons by shape and size and color and design and material—and especially to count them! I could even put all the information into a graph or a table—really look at the data!

But this is not the right time to become a button expert. My job now is to get ready for social studies.

Tomorrow.

5

Show-and-Tell

When it's time for social studies Tuesday morning, I lay everything on the table that Mrs. Casey moved to the front of the room: the bobbins, the pens, the gear, the doorknob, the scissors, the hammer, the thimble, the needles, and the antique eyeglasses. I have a small assortment of buttons, and I empty them out carefully at one end of the table. It all makes an interesting display, like you'd see at a museum. Or an antiques store.

Or my room.

I talk for a minute or so, and tell everyone what Grampa told me about the history of the mill, and I explain how the things on the table came from different times during its life.

Mrs. Casey asks the class to gather around, and as they do, she picks up the scissors.

My stomach tightens up like a little fist, and I think I might have just made a bad face. Because from now on, whenever I look at those scissors, I'm going to have to remember *two* things—my wonderful afternoon with Grampa, and Mrs. Casey's pink fingernail polish.

She opens and closes the long blades, and they make this great metallic swish, ending with a sharp *snap*.

"A tailor must have used these to cut through several layers of wool or cotton at the same time—I have never seen shears this large before!"

Following Mrs. Casey's lead, the kids start touching and inspecting everything—just what I was afraid would happen. But I don't really blame them. This old stuff is irresistible, like holding a hundred years with one hand.

Then, a complete surprise—a bunch of kids start going nuts about the buttons.

"A button shaped like a *tomato*?"

"There's a ship on this one!"

"Look at this super-bright yellow—I *love* it!"

"A starfish . . . and there's a baseball!"

"That gold one with the eagle? It's gotta be off an army uniform."

"*Oooh*—diamonds!"

With all the bright colors, and some of them glittering in the pile? The buttons look sort of like jewels that spilled from a treasure chest.

Everyone keeps poking through them until Mrs. Casey says, "Thank you for sharing all this, Grace. Let's get back to our seats now, and please take out your notes from the homework reading."

The Burnham Mills show is over, just like that.

I gather up my stuff, and in another fifteen minutes it'll be lunchtime. It's as if my show-and-tell never happened. Which is just fine with me.

A second surprise comes about a half hour later in the cafeteria.

Taylor says, "Do you have those buttons with you? Could I look at them again?"

From the end of our lunch table, Hank pipes up, "Me too!"

So I take the bag out of my backpack and pour the buttons onto an empty cafeteria tray. As the tray slides down the center of the table, everyone leans in to look and touch—everyone except Ellie.

She nods at the tray and says, "My mom used to do all kinds of sewing and knitting and quilting, and so did both of my grandmothers. We've got a drawer at home that's loaded with buttons—a *lot* more than that."

Taylor says, "We've got buttons at home, too, but these are *way* better!"

Brooke nods. "I've seen some buttons at my house, too."

"Hey—I've got an idea," Ellie says. "How about if we all bring some buttons tomorrow? We can look at them after lunch, just to see what everyone has."

This moment? This is the right moment for me to say,

The truth is, no matter how many buttons anybody else has, I've got way more!

But I don't say a word, and the other kids at the table are saying, "Yeah," and "I could find some buttons," and "Cool!" and "Count me in!"

And I can't help thinking that if *I* had made this suggestion? Everyone would have thought it was dorky—especially Ellie.

As I bag up my buttons for the second time today, I understand what's happening. Ellie likes to be the one who has the most and the best of everything. She isn't too obnoxious about it, not usually.

But I've seen her act this way before.

I know *exactly* why Ellie suggested that all the kids at our table should bring some buttons to lunch tomorrow—and this is not just a theory. It's because Ellie is totally sure that *she* has the most and the best and the prettiest buttons in the universe, and she wants to prove that to everybody.

But, of course, Ellie *doesn't* have the most or the best or the prettiest.

I do . . . probably.

And maybe for the first time ever.

I think about this the whole rest of the school day. And even as I'm doing my homework after dinner, Ellie and her buttons are right here inside my head.

So, just before bed, I begin filling plastic sandwich bags with buttons. I'm aiming for quality, variety, and especially *quantity*.

I stop at eight bags. That ought to do it.

Because if Ellie tries to turn tomorrow's lunchtime into a big show-off session, then she's going to get a surprise.

From me.

6

Strange Galaxy

It's second period on Wednesday, and Hank whispers to me. Again.

I can't tell what he said, but I nod anyway. Again.

We're sitting in the front row of the auditorium, and I'm turned halfway around in my seat so I can see the other kids as they arrive for our first sixth-grade assembly. I need Hank to stop bothering me because I'm on a mission—counting buttons. And also keeping a running total in my head.

. . . 341 . . . 349 . . . 352 . . . 355 . . .

When I can't quite see, I have to estimate:

flannel or long-sleeve shirt—eight buttons
button-front sweater or short-sleeve shirt—six buttons
pullover polo shirt—three buttons
pants or shorts—one button, maybe two
skirt—one button
T-shirts, sweatshirts, or sweatpants—zero buttons

Hank pokes me with his elbow.

"Mrs. Lang is looking at you—here she comes!"

I hear him, but I keep counting anyway.

"Grace! Face forward! This is *not* the time or the place for socializing."

Under my breath I say, "Three hundred sixty-three," and then I turn and sit back in my seat.

I look up at Mrs. Lang. "Sorry . . . except I wasn't socializing. I was collecting data."

She frowns and shakes her head. "Eyes front. That's our assembly rule."

I always feel sorry for teachers at assemblies. It seems like they're trying to show the principal and all the other teachers how *their* kids are just about perfect.

But that's only a theory.

Mrs. Lang walks on, her clipboard gripped in the crook of her arm. And I notice that she's wearing pants, a collared shirt, and a sweater—at least fifteen buttons.

I want to turn around again, to try to pick up my button count, but I don't dare. It's too early in the school year to risk getting on Mrs. Lang's bad side—I've got her for homeroom, plus math and science. Although maybe Mrs. Lang doesn't really *have* a good side. Then it wouldn't matter, right?

Another interesting theory, but I don't want to test it—not today.

Instead, I try to estimate how much of the sixth grade had already arrived in the auditorium when Mrs. Lang made me stop counting . . . probably about two-thirds.

So, if the first *two*-thirds of the kids were wearing

about three hundred and sixty buttons, then the remaining *one*-third of the kids would be wearing about half that many: another one hundred and eighty. Which means that today, the whole sixth grade is wearing . . . five hundred and forty buttons. Approximately.

Of course, those are just the buttons on the clothes the kids are wearing right now. There are lots more buttons on all their other clothes at home—the shirts and pants and jeans and shorts in dresser drawers, plus the skirts and other clothes on hangers and hooks in closets. And then there are the buttons on everybody's coats and jackets and raincoats.

To get a scientific count of the sixth graders' buttons, I would have to ask every kid to go home, study all their clothes, count every button, and then fill out a form for me.

Which isn't going to happen.

Besides, this sudden urge to count buttons? I know it's only a distraction, something I'm doing to keep myself from worrying about what might happen at lunchtime—right after this assembly.

I almost never wake up early, but this morning at six-fifteen I sat straight up in bed, sweating. I'd been dreaming about snowboarding down a mountainside, and then an avalanche broke loose above me, and suddenly that rushing hillside of snow turned into a towering wave of buttons, trying to sweep me under, bury me.

And the moment I got myself fully awake? I started to worry about lunch.

And buttons.

And the Ellie Effect.

My thoughts keep spinning, and I begin to wonder how many buttons there are on the clothes of the *other* kids at school today. And the teachers, too.

And beyond the school, there are the parents of the kids, at home or at work, with buttons on *their* clothes. Plus all the rest of the people of this town . . . and this state . . . and this country, and this continent, and this hemisphere, and this planet!

And what about the buttons on all the clothes on all the bodies buried in all the graveyards, everywhere in the world? Gross . . . but true. That would add up to billions and billions more!

I feel dizzy, and I tip my head back and stare up at the ceiling of the auditorium. It's like I've accidentally pointed a telescope toward a strange galaxy, and instead of stars and planets, I'm looking into an endless new sky filled with buttons.

The assembly begins, and the principal is at the podium onstage, waiting as the room gets quiet.

"Your teachers and I have known many of you for more than five years, and we are so excited about the amazing year we've planned. It's going to be demanding, and so far, you're doing great! As all of us look ahead together, I'm hoping that . . ."

Mrs. Porter keeps talking, but I'm having trouble listening. My hands are cold, and it feels like I have a knot in the center of my stomach.

I hate getting upset about anything, but to feel this upset about *buttons*? It's not even logical. Because, really, who cares about buttons? No one ever even *thinks* about buttons!

Unless one pops off and your pants fall down.

I saw that in a cartoon, but there's no reason why it couldn't happen in real life: A button pops, gravity pulls, and pants fall—it's basic science, simple cause and effect.

Cause and effect!

The first time I heard that phrase was during a second-grade science lesson. It means that nothing happens without a reason. It means that events can always be studied and understood. Which is so . . . comforting.

And suddenly I am absolutely sure that what I need here is more scientific thinking—more understanding.

And less emotion.

Except . . . right now? I understand the cause of my worries perfectly—and the anxious feelings are only getting worse. Why? As soon as this assembly is over, I know that I'm going to stop by my locker, grab a backpack full of buttons, and then go to the cafeteria with my best friend.

Whether my stomach likes it or not.

7

Buttons for Lunch

At our table in the cafeteria, the eating part of the lunch period is over quickly.

Since the main event was Ellie's idea, she takes charge. Which is what I thought would happen.

"Let's get the table cleared off—"

"Yeah, but maybe keep your trays."

That's Hank—interrupting Ellie. She shoots a look at him before continuing.

"And yes, keep a tray if you want to."

Once everyone is back and settled, Ellie says, "I think Grace should go first. Then we can go on around the table to the left. So, besides the buttons you had yesterday, did you find any others at home?"

"Uh . . . yes."

I'm lost, scattered, totally flustered.

Because *my* plan was to wait until everyone else was done, and then dump out bag after bag of buttons, and calmly enjoy everyone's amazement—especially Ellie's.

And now I don't know what to do. Plus my stomach is still hurting.

I reach into my backpack and pull out one bag—a mix of green, blue, red, and yellow buttons, all about the size of a nickel.

"I . . . I have these."

I pour the buttons onto a tray and slide it to my left.

And in a flash, I see why Ellie started things off this way—so that *her* buttons will be the last ones revealed!

Ellie smiles at my tray. "Nice colors," she says.

But to me it sounds like she's only being polite.

Cody is on my left, and from the pocket of his hoodie he pulls out a dark blue sock with a bulge down in the toe.

"*Eww*—that's gross!" Taylor slides as far away from Cody as she can get.

"What? It's not stinky, if that's what you're worried about. And in case you didn't know it, plastic bags are *terrible* for the environment."

Cody empties his buttons onto a tray, then stuffs the sock back into his pocket. There are four or five bright orange ones, three large red ones, several dozen in different shades of gray and tan, fifteen or twenty black ones, and then lots of smaller white buttons.

To my eye, the most interesting buttons on his tray are the largest black ones. They have an anchor-and-rope design cut into the surface. I've got thirty or forty like that.

I point at one. "I'm pretty sure that's a US Navy button."

Cody picks it up. "Yeah, that's what my mom said.

These were on my dad's old jacket, but he burned a big hole in it on a fishing trip, and she only kept the buttons."

And that's it for Cody.

Taylor starts pulling small plastic bags out of her backpack. "When my mom was in junior high, she and her big sister got into decorating stuff with buttons—lampshades and coasters and glass jars, all kinds of things. We still have some of the coasters. And my mom kept all the buttons they never used. I'm not allowed to get them mixed together. We've got some other regular buttons, too, but I didn't bring them."

There are at least fifteen bags on Taylor's tray, and even though the colors are different, the buttons look identical, each a little bigger than the kind used on the front of a shirt.

Kevin is next, and his buttons aren't in a plastic bag or a sock. He just pulls a few handfuls from his pockets.

"These are from the sewing box in our family room. There are more, but I was almost late for the bus this morning, so . . . that's it."

These look a lot like Cody's mix, only I don't spot any US Navy buttons. But I do see four that are made of pewter. They all have the same raised design on the surface—a swan.

It's Hank's turn, and he stands up and spreads out five white sheets of poster board, each one a little bigger than a regular piece of printer paper. Every sheet has buttons on it, mounted in rows and columns, and every button is fastened in place with thin black wire threaded into holes poked through the board.

"I searched for all the loose buttons at my house yesterday, and then I got them organized, first by color, then by shape and size. And also by the number of holes they have—two or four . . . except for the buttons like this brass one, and this little round-topped blue one. This kind just has a single loop on the back. I recorded how many of each separate kind I have—that's the number I wrote underneath some of them. And I mounted the buttons like this because I looked online, and this is sort of how collectors organize them. I'm not really done yet."

Everyone is kind of blown away by Hank's presentation, but I'm not surprised. Hank and I teamed up for the fourth-grade science fair. When we were working at his house one Saturday, I saw his butterfly and moth collection—over a hundred and fifty different species, from tiny ones with delicate white wings, to a brilliant green luna moth bigger than my dad's hand. Each insect was perfectly mounted and labeled.

Six or seven other kids have come over to stand around our table, some from my homeroom and others from Mr. Scott's and Mrs. Casey's rooms—a few fifth graders, too. Everyone is leaning forward, and they remind me of a quiet audience at one of those golf tournaments on TV.

Brooke and Diana didn't bring a lot—about as many as Kevin. The most interesting thing on either of their trays is some cloth-covered buttons Brooke found.

Finally, it's Ellie's turn.

We've got at least twelve extra spectators now, and she smiles at them and says, "Sorry there's not enough room for you to sit at the table, but I hope you can see everything anyway. First of all, I have some military buttons, which are *very* special."

Ellie pauses, making sure she has our full attention.

"My great-great-grandfather joined the United States Army in 1918, and then after World War One he stayed in the army until he became a captain. And these are buttons off some of his clothes. These huge ones are from a heavy overcoat. The oldest buttons, these brown metal ones? They were actually on his uniform when he was fighting in France during the war. And these shiny brass ones came from his captain's uniform later on. Now, these six buttons? They're from a US Marine uniform that my grandmother's brother wore. I never met him, because he died in the Vietnam War, when my grandmother was still in high school. I'll pass them around, but please don't take them out of the protective bag."

Ellie has used two different cafeteria trays now, and she has five more stacked in front of her—she's got a whole little show planned out, like something on the History Channel! I don't know whether to be impressed or annoyed or jealous, so all three feelings are banging around inside me.

And Ellie keeps going.

"These nine buttons? They're from my great-aunt Ellen's wedding dress—she's the person I'm named for. See how they shine when you tilt them? They're made from this semiprecious stone called white opal. Aunt Ellen gave them to my mom so that *I* could wear them someday on *my* wedding dress, and I didn't even know that until last night—so *amazing*!"

The wedding dress buttons, also in plastic, get to parade down the table on a tray of their own.

"I think these might be my favorites. My dad told me that back in 1898, his great-grandparents bought a farm in southern Illinois. And these two buttons came from a pair of overalls that my great-great-grandfather wore almost every day!"

Ellie passes them to me. They're made of brass, and raised up on the front of each button are two words: STRONG HOLD. I want to ask her what else she knows about her great-great-grandparents, but Ellie's not slowing down for anything.

"Okay, so these twelve shiny black buttons? They're carved from a stone called onyx, and my mom told me how she wore them on a long blue gown."

There's a muffled laugh to my left, but it's not about Ellie's show. Kevin and Cody have moved so they're sitting next to each other, and my tray is between them. They're piling up buttons, seeing who can build the tallest stack before it topples.

Ellie looks, too, and she pauses to frown at them. But the guys don't stop. She's taking too long, and she knows it.

"I've got this one last thing. My grandmother on my

mother's side of the family? After my grandfather died, she took all his wool business suits and used the cloth to make a big quilt, and I've seen it—mostly gray and blue and brown, kind of ugly. But she also kept every single button from all those suits. And here they are. And . . . and it's like all I have left of my grandfather now is this little bag of buttons. Don't you think that's just so . . . *sad*?"

It gets very still.

Kevin, Taylor, Brooke, Hank—all the kids around the lunch table are genuinely moved by what Ellie just said.

I feel a little choked up, too . . . and kind of ashamed.

Because I've been sitting here, gritting my teeth while Ellie does her dramatic, super-expanded show-and-tell, and I'm feeling like she's showing off—and, of course, Ellie *is* showing off.

But this moment? It's a side of her I haven't seen very often, maybe only three or four times in all the days we've spent hanging around together. And what made Ellie get so thoughtful and full of feelings? Some old buttons—which is totally strange!

But it's also touching, and sort of sweet. And seeing that? It's a good reminder that Ellie knows how to be sweet—when she wants to be. And this makes me happy in a way I hadn't expected.

Ellie knows she just hit the high point of her big show.

"So, all these other buttons? They're just from sewing projects and stuff."

As Ellie pours the contents of a large Tupperware container onto her last two trays, I can tell that a lot of these buttons are nicer than the ones other kids had—probably just from more expensive clothes.

Maybe from Paris—like her sneakers.

And now I'm mad at myself for getting all snarky and jealous. Again.

Because that's the problem—Ellie keeps making me feel this way.

And, of course, this is my perfect opportunity to make *her* feel jealous. About fifteen other kids are standing around our table now, and I've got a chance to one-up the one-uppiest girl in the world, to show that Ellie does *not* have the most and the best and the prettiest, not this time.

All I have to do is reach down into my backpack, pull out seven other plastic bags, and then drop my button bomb—a massive assortment of colors and designs and sizes—*KA-BOOM!*

But I don't.

It doesn't feel like something a best friend would do, that's all—or even just a friend. And it isn't like Ellie put on her little show to *try* to make me feel jealous. She's just being . . . herself.

And besides all that? I still kind of like this feeling that I've got a secret. It's like I'm super rich, and no one else has a clue.

"Hey, Grace—Cody and I are trying to figure out a game here, and we need six green buttons and six blue ones. Do you maybe want to swap some buttons with us?"

The question catches me by surprise, and I hear myself saying, "Um . . . no, that's okay—just go ahead and take the ones you want. I've got a lot there."

"*Really?* Thanks!"

"So, could I have four, but all different colors?" It's James Kinney, one of the kids from Mr. Scott's homeroom.

"Sure," I say, and then some other kids jump right in.

"Could *I* have four?"

"How about five?"

I'm almost laughing now. "Anybody who wants to can take up to *six* buttons from my tray, okay?"

And right away, everybody waits for a turn to take six, including all the spectators. Plus Ellie.

Then Ellie says, "And . . . um, if anybody wants to take one . . . or maybe two buttons from my last trays right here, go ahead. Because my mom said I could do whatever I want with them."

And everybody takes one or two, including all the spectators. Plus me.

Some other kids begin drifting over to see what's going on, and as Ellie quickly gathers up her buttons, she says, "I'm really glad I thought of this. It was kind of fun, don't you think?"

A few kids smile at her, but most of them are still gathered around my tray, trying to decide if they picked the right buttons, or if they should trade some in for different colors. The tray is almost empty.

Four minutes later, when the bell rings, I walk out of the cafeteria, headed for math class with Mrs. Lang. And I've got the strongest feeling that *something* just happened—but I'm not sure what.

So I lay out the facts, which are simple: A bunch of kids looked at a bunch of buttons from a bunch of different homes and places, and then a bunch *more* kids gathered around to watch.

Another fact: When I offered some free buttons, nobody refused. *Everybody* took six buttons, and also one or two of Ellie's.

So ... right now, more than twenty kids are walking around school with seven or eight buttons clicking in their pockets—buttons none of them even knew they wanted until a few minutes ago!

Another odd fact? It felt so easy to give most of mine away—actually, I just waved goodbye to about a hundred and thirty buttons!

But Ellie? She really didn't want to give away even *one* of hers.

How come? That's simple, too: Ellie's buttons have history. They mean something to her—the way the smooth gray stone on my dresser means something to me. But those boxes of buttons from Grampa's mill? To me, they're just . . . buttons.

The main fact? These completely ordinary little objects seem to be changing right in front of my eyes.

But how?

And why?

That's not clear—so I'm going to need more data.

The only thing I'm pretty sure of? Whatever's going on, it's not over.

As I walk into Mrs. Lang's room, I notice one more fact: My stomach is feeling perfectly fine.

8

Total Geniuses

"**H**i, Mom, I'm home."

She calls back from her office upstairs, which is more like a big closet. "Hi, sweetheart. I've got a Skype meeting in about ten minutes—get yourself a snack, okay?"

"Okay."

I go to the kitchen, but food is the last thing on my mind. I open the door to the laundry room, then dig around inside the broom closet until I find the sewing box that Ben and I gave Mom for Mother's Day four years ago.

Mom doesn't sew for fun or as a hobby or anything like that. But she does have some basic sewing stuff. She used to keep it all in a couple of plastic containers from a Chinese restaurant—until we got her this deluxe, denim-covered sewing box. It still looks brand-new.

I open the lid and lift out a plastic tray loaded with spools of thread. And then, under a large pincushion and three packets of needles, beneath a package of iron-on patches and some loops of flat elastic, way down on the very bottom of the sewing box, I find what I'm looking for: loose buttons.

Ben comes into the kitchen about fifteen minutes later. "Um . . . what's going on here?"

"I'm recording family history."

"Actually, I'm *pretty* sure that you're taking pictures of buttons."

I straighten up and wave my hand over the table. "See this? Mom and Dad have been married for nineteen and a half years, and these are the family's unattached buttons—the Hamlin Family Button Collection. There are one hundred and thirty-four of them. That works out to about seven buttons for each year they've been married."

I pause to let the information sink in.

"Okay, I'm with you."

"Of course, I really wish I knew the *order* the buttons had been saved in, so I could make an exact timeline from the very first button, right up to the most recent one. But I don't know that—and wishing is not scientific. And I also don't know which buttons came from whose clothes, except for a few. See these five pewter buttons with the rose design? They used to be on that red-and-white handmade sweater Mom has, but then one got lost. So she snipped off these five and tossed them in with the sewing junk, then sewed six new matching buttons back onto her sweater. I could probably figure out what year that happened. . . ."

I turn to Ben. "Do you think Mom and Dad started finding more stray buttons once they had you and me?"

"Makes sense—more people, more clothes, more buttons."

He picks up a large silver button with a harp design stamped onto the metal.

"This one is mine, for sure. I lost a button off my middle school band uniform. Mr. Clift made me buy a new one, and Mom taught me how to sew it on myself. Then about a year later she found a button under the cushions of the family room couch. And here it is."

That gets me thinking. "You know, every single button here has some kind of a story."

Ben squints at me. "Well, yeah . . . but I bet a lot of these were just extra buttons that came with a pair of pants or a sweater or something. Not much of a story."

I'm not giving up. "But every button's story started *way* before any of them got to our house, onto our clothes. Because all these buttons had to get designed by somebody, and then each one got made somewhere, right? And then each one got moved around by people and then sewn onto something, or dropped one by one into tiny plastic bags and stuck inside the back pocket of some new pants—right?"

"Yeah," Ben says, "except stuff like that happens to *everything*—like this chair, or my shoes, or that lightbulb. Every single thing in the whole world has a story of how it got made and how it got to be somewhere. And a button is just one other thing."

"Okay," I say, "but tell me this: If you stop using a

lightbulb, do you put it in a box in the broom closet and leave it there for *nineteen and a half years*?"

"No. . . ."

"So there *is* something different about buttons, right?"

"Yes, because when you stop using a lightbulb, it's probably because it doesn't work anymore, so why keep it? But a button can always do what it was made to do, unless it gets crushed or broken in half or something. Which doesn't happen much. Put an old shirt button onto a *different* shirt, and it'll still work."

"Exactly!" Then I pause a second to get the next bit right. "And *that's* why people hang on to buttons, even if there's no way they'll ever use them again. They don't keep them to use them; they keep them because they *might*!"

It feels like I've just solved a mystery.

Ben nods, stroking his chin as if he had a beard. "And I guess figuring out all this proves once more that *we* are a couple of total geniuses!"

I laugh and then say, "Except *I'm* the one who has twenty-seven boxes full of buttons in my bedroom, and *you* don't. Which probably makes me a little bit *more* of a total genius than you are."

"Interesting theory," he says. "But having twenty-seven boxes of buttons in your bedroom *probably* just means that you're a crackpot!"

"Hmm . . . you could be right." Then I remember something. "Oh! Could you do me a favor? Please don't tell anybody that I've got all those buttons, okay?"

"How come?" he asks, but then quickly whispers, "Ohhh, right—the crackpot thing. Don't worry. Your secret is safe with me. And, like, if you want to tiptoe upstairs and live in Mom and Dad's attic for the rest of your life? I'm cool with that, too."

I cross my eyes and stick out my tongue.

Then I turn back to the kitchen table and use my phone to take some more pictures.

Of buttons.

9

Button Fever

It's Thursday, and I wake up thinking about buttons. Again.

How many do I actually have? Which color do I have the most of? How many of each size do I have? Of all the buttons I have, which has the largest diameter . . . and the smallest?

Then I remember what Ben said to me yesterday in the kitchen, and I think, *Maybe Ben's right—maybe I really am a crackpot!*

Forty-five minutes later, I feel even more like an oddball, because right before I leave the house to go to the bus stop, I run upstairs to my room, grab a big handful of cranberry-red buttons, and toss them into my backpack. I just feel like I want to have some buttons with me at school today.

Which is definitely strange.

But as I drop into a seat near the back of the bus, I

discover that my strange condition is not unique. Because in the row right in front of me, four boys are arguing—about buttons.

"Are you kidding? Metal buttons are *always* better than plastic—anybody knows that. And if a metal one is off some kind of a uniform? That's the *best*—end of discussion!"

"Okay . . . but what if you had a plastic one shaped like the *Millennium Falcon* or something? I think that'd be *lots* better than some old metal button."

"Well, maybe—but you're never gonna see *that* in your whole life!"

Another kid has his phone out. "Hey—look at this!"

They huddle around the screen, and one of them reads aloud: " 'Handmade *Millennium Falcon* Button'? Whoa! I'd trade an army button for *that* thing, any day!"

"There's a Chewbacca button, too! And R2-D2 . . . and *Darth Vader*! That is so *cool*!"

But the thing that *I* think is cool? Not one of these guys was anywhere near my lunch table yesterday, and none of them are in Mrs. Casey's social studies class either!

How come they're talking about buttons?

I walk myself through it:

Okay, by the end of lunchtime yesterday, let's say there were twenty-two kids around our table, and probably half of them were boys, and each one walked away thinking about buttons, plus each had seven or eight new buttons in his pocket. And let's say those eleven guys each

mentioned buttons or showed some to three other guys.
Then that would be thirty-three more boys—and if each
of them mentioned buttons to three or four others, then,
just like that, we're up to more than a hundred guys with
a brand-new interest in buttons!

It's a decent theory, but I need to test it.

"Excuse me. . . . I heard what you guys were saying just now. How come you're talking about buttons?"

The boy with the phone turns and looks at me.

"Everybody's talking about them, that's all."

"Everybody? But, like, what got *you* started talking about buttons?"

He stares at me. "I don't know. Who cares?"

"*I* care. I'd just like to know." And I smile at him.

A different boy says, "What, are you the Button Police or something?"

A kid laughs and says, "*Look out,* it's the Button Squad!"

Another guy snarls in a deep voice, "All right, you punks—up against the wall, and hand over all your buttons!"

They keep goofing and laughing, and some of the other boys near the back of the bus join in.

So, I guess this has turned into an experiment about guys showing off for each other. Or maybe just showing off for me.

But science keeps marching forward, no matter what.

And I remember something that might be useful.

I reach into the bottom of my book bag, grab some buttons, and face the boys again.

"Hey—Phone Guy!"

The kid looks up from his screen. "What?"

I hold out my hand. "These aren't metal, but I've got some questions, and I'll give you two of these *blood-red* buttons for each question you can answer. Deal?"

Now I've got the whole group's attention.

The kid with the phone smiles. "Sure, deal."

"Okay. So, when did you start thinking about buttons?"

"Yesterday . . . in the afternoon."

"How come?"

"This guy, James Kinney? He's in my art class, and he started sliding some buttons around on our table, making shapes and patterns and stuff, and then all of us started using them like little air-hockey pucks, just messing around. And everybody thought they were cool."

"Great—that's all I wanted to know. Thanks."

And I drop four blood-red buttons into his outstretched hand—a very small price to pay for totally proving a theory!

I stay on high alert during the rest of my ride to school, and also as I walk through the halls after we arrive. And I observe *six* more conversations about buttons!

When I get to homeroom, I'm a little out of breath. I look for Ellie—she's over by the windows with Taylor, Brooke, and Diana.

"Hi, guys. You'll never guess what happened on my bus! I was—"

"Wait!" Ellie says, and then she sticks her arm in front of my eyes. "What do you think?"

She has a bracelet on her wrist—and it's made of small white buttons.

Brooke says, "Isn't it beautiful?"

Taylor adds, "And the buttons are all made out of seashells, right?"

Ellie nods. "They're mother-of-pearl. All I did was string them like little flat beads onto this thin elastic cord. And now I can stretch it on and off, just like a candy charm bracelet. Here. . . ."

Ellie rolls it off, lifts my left hand, and slips it onto my wrist.

I hold out my arm and study the bracelet.

Again, Ellie has surprised me. I can't remember her ever doing something creative like this.

"It looks great on you! Do you want to keep it until lunch?"

"It's really pretty, but I think you should wear it," I say, and hand it to her.

"Okay."

I can see Ellie's glad I gave her bracelet back.

Then Taylor says, "Hey—you started to tell us something . . . about your bus, right?"

"Oh, that? It wasn't important."

Which isn't quite true.

But I'm thinking like a scientist now—at least, I'm trying to.

Because I want to see if kids are behaving in a certain way, and also why. So, should I go around talking about this particular condition that I'm analyzing? No, because that could start changing the results of my own study—which is bad science, especially if I talk about this condition with people who I think already *have* the condition I'm observing.

And these girls? They absolutely *have* the condition—they've got button fever!

I mean, I've got button fever, too. But here's the thing: I *know* I've got it.

Ellie, Taylor, Brooke, and Diana? They're like those boys on the bus: They've got it, but they don't really know it.

Not yet.

Once the day begins, I stay close to Ellie whenever we have classes together or when I see her in the halls and at lunch. Each time she shows her bracelet to someone, or each time someone notices it or asks about it, I make a detailed note.

Ellie is never shy about showing off something new or special, and she has a *lot* of friends. By the time she steps onto her bus Thursday afternoon, I have observed thirty-nine girls and twelve boys in grades four, five, and six who each got an up-close look at Ellie's bracelet—that's *fifty-one* kids!

Of course, there's no quick way to know what those fifty-one kids thought about Ellie's bracelet, or whether any of those kids might have told any *other* kids about it. And I'm sure Ellie showed her bracelet to some additional kids when I wasn't around.

Even so, I think I've got enough data to support a very simple theory: Avery Elementary School is going to see a *dramatic* increase of button fever.

And it will probably happen soon.

10

Bitten by the Button Bug

Before I even find a seat on the bus Friday morning, the boy from yesterday, the one with the phone, gets right up in my face, talking fast.

"Those buttons? The red ones you gave me? You got any more of those? I found some really big green buttons, and I'll trade 'em for some more of those red ones, if you want to. What do you say, huh? You want to trade?"

"Um, let me sit down first, okay?"

I live pretty close to school, so the bus is nearly full, and as I walk back to look for a seat, I'm in the middle of a massive swap session, with kids calling to each other.

"I've got fifteen little white buttons here, perfect for making a bracelet or something, and I'm looking for buttons made of pewter. Anybody have any pewter?"

"No pewter, but I've got a really nice brass one."

"Brass? Does it have an eagle on it?"

"No, it has a globe."

"I'll take it! What do you want for it?"

"What've you got? I'm looking for some of those US Navy buttons, the kind with the anchor."

"Pewter? Who's looking for pewter?"

"I am!"

Phone Boy is still with me when I sit down.

"So, those red ones? You have any?"

"First of all, my name is Grace—what's yours?"

"Chris."

"How come you want more red buttons?"

"That color? It's really rare. I've got my eye on a couple of Coast Guard buttons, but I've got to get some good ammo before I try to make a trade. So, I was thinking that these two big green guys ought to be worth about *eight* of your red ones—what do you say?"

"Hey, *I* want some of those red ones! Look at these yellow buttons—*fantastic* color, right?"

It's the boy who was joking about the Button Police yesterday, and the four yellow buttons he's offering to trade? They're *mine*—some of the buttons I gave away from my tray at lunch on Wednesday! Which means *he* must have gotten them from someone who was at our table . . . except, really, those buttons could have already changed hands five or six times!

The driver slams the bus to a stop and waves some cars past. Then she stands up and yells, "*Get in your seats and stay there! Any more moving around when the bus is rolling, and I'll call the school and have the principal meet us at the curb—you got that?*"

Everyone sits down fast, and there's a lot of nodding,

and it's quiet. But the moment the bus moves, the yelling and the trading picks up again—with kids sitting now.

The boy, Chris, hands me his two green buttons. "Nice, huh?"

They're very large, at least an inch and a half across, and there's a carved design on each one, sort of a notch on the front that cuts across the two holes.

"Hold them up," he says. "See how the light comes right through? Almost like glass or something. Really great buttons!"

Even though I have so, so many buttons, I haven't seen any like this pair, not yet. And all of a sudden I really want them!

But without even thinking, I pretend I don't.

"Yeah . . . I mean, they're *okay,* I guess. But *eight* of my red ones? For two? I don't think so."

"How about seven?"

And now I know I've got him hooked.

"I could trade six, I guess."

"Okay, six! *Deal!*"

I dig around in the bottom of my book bag, and hand over six of my best blood-red buttons. Our deal is complete, and I have never felt like this, never in my whole life! Trading is so *fun*!

I hear myself calling out, "Who's got those pewter buttons?"

"Back here—I've got three. Pass these up to her."

It's a girl two rows behind me, and I think she's a fifth grader.

I study the buttons, and then I frown. "Oh—they're not the same. That's too bad."

"Right," she says, "but they're all snowflake designs . . . and every snowflake is different, right? So, they're still pretty amazing."

I can tell this girl's smart.

I say, "Yeah, but I like it when buttons match. Like these cranberry-red buttons? I've got enough that somebody could actually sew them onto a sweater. Such a great color!" And I pass three of them back to her. "I think I've got six, maybe even seven . . . if you wanted to trade."

These pewter buttons in my hand have a very nice weight to them—so solid. And just like with the big green ones, I feel like I've *got* to own these buttons!

I can tell the girl's not sold yet, so I say, "I'll tell you what. How about I give you *three* of my red ones for each one of these. Deal?"

And now this girl knows that she's got *me* on the hook! And she knows that I know that she knows.

"Hmm . . . I think maybe *four* of your red ones for each of mine would be better—twelve total. How about that?"

"Twelve for three? Okay . . . but you're getting a *really* good deal!"

I hunt around to find nine more red buttons, and I pass them back. Even though I feel like I got beat on this deal, I don't care. These pewter buttons feel so heavy, so *real*!

I'm getting low on my red buttons, so I'm done

trading—for now. But I've got *seven* other little sandwich bags of buttons in my locker, the ones I didn't show at lunch on Wednesday! I must have a couple thousand buttons there, all kinds! If I'm careful, I could probably get my hands on every single pewter button at school today, probably even get—

My mind screeches to a halt.

What is wrong with me?

I've been hearing this hyper little voice inside my head, and it's like I don't know who's talking!

Because standing at the bus stop five minutes ago? I was Grace Hamlin, the careful scientist. I was all set to observe and analyze and take some notes. I was going to see if there were any new cases of button fever today. Then I got on the bus, and in ten seconds I morphed into a wild button zombie—*Must get more buttons!*

A sudden sharp stillness fills my thinking. I look around me on the bus, and now I can see what's going on here.

It's clear that not everybody has buttons—probably only about fifteen kids are actually trading. But every kid on the bus is totally tuned in, following each transaction and choosing sides, too—there's a cheering section for every trade.

"Don't do it! Your button is *way* better than that piece of junk he's trying to give you!"

And something else: The kids who *don't* have any buttons? They wish they did. And by Monday morning, my theory is that most of them will.

That thought I had a minute ago, that I should rush to my locker and grab some button bags, and keep on trading like mad?

I can't do that—no way!

Because if I did, everyone would figure out that I've got a massive supply of amazing buttons. They would see that I have this huge advantage.

And they would probably think it wasn't fair.

Which is true . . . I guess.

So I'd better just be an observer here, a scientist. Which is not the same as being in the action. It feels more like being a spy.

I tell myself that I can do this, that I can stay outside the flow. I'm going to be scientific: I'm going to watch the events and keep trying to understand what's going on.

That's what I tell myself.

But as I get off the bus with three pewter buttons in my right hand and the two big green ones in my left hand? I am so *glad* that these buttons are *mine*!

And I admit that it might be tough to stay true to my scientific goals.

Because that feeling of making a great trade? It's a hard thing to forget.

11

Fashion and Power

When I get to homeroom and look around, buttons are everywhere.

But this is not like the wild scene on the bus, because our teacher is sitting at her desk typing on her laptop, and even before the day officially begins, Mrs. Lang expects everyone to be well behaved and orderly.

Still, there are several pockets of intense activity. And who's in the middle of the action? Ellie.

Which doesn't surprise me.

When Ellie sees me, she waves for me to come over, a huge smile on her face. She's wearing her new button bracelet for the second day in a row.

"Guess what: A lot of kids asked me about my bracelet yesterday, so I made some more last night!"

Again, not a surprise.

"First, I sorted all my buttons, that big batch my mom gave me. I did colors and then size. I mean, I love this first bracelet, but it used up *way* too many buttons. So I had to figure out how to make them last, you know? And look, I made *five* of these!"

She hands me a piece of thin red ribbon. It's about half an inch wide and about six inches long, and it's made of cloth—like a hair ribbon. Eight small white buttons are sewn onto it, spaced evenly along the length. At one end of the ribbon there's a short loop of heavy white thread.

"You put it on this way, see?"

Ellie wraps the ribbon around my wrist, and then fastens it by putting the last button on one end through the white loop on the other. And now I'm wearing a red-ribbon-button bracelet.

Ellie's sewing isn't going to win any prizes, but this bracelet? It's sweet and simple, and *very* cute!

As she helps me take it off my wrist, she keeps talking.

"So, I decided that my goal for today is to trade my bracelets for as many really *big* buttons as I can get. And so far, I've got these seven—with *three* bracelets still left to trade! Pretty good, huh?"

She holds out her hand and shows me seven gorgeous buttons, each about the size of the green ones I got on the bus. Three of them are made from some kind of pale blue seashell. One is bright orange plastic, two are speckled like a brownish bird's egg, and the last button looks like it's made of pale yellow glass with bubbles in it—but it's plastic.

So Ellie's plan? It's working really, really well!

But she's not the only one with ideas. Because this morning? Buttons are the new fashion accessory.

Following Ellie's lead, five other girls have some kind of a button bracelet—I think Ellie's new one is still the best. Three girls have a fancy button or two strung onto a cord or a chain and worn as a necklace. One girl has sewn a bright yellow button onto each belt loop of her jeans! And Taylor? She's got one little blue button on each of her white sneakers, sewn onto the laces somehow, and centered about halfway up—it's an interesting look.

In the back corner, four boys have these strange bunches of buttons hanging from their belts. But I wouldn't call this fashion—more like . . . advertising.

And it's working, because I walk right over for a closer look.

"Hey, Cody, can I check out that bunch of black buttons?" And I point at a group on his left hip.

"Sure."

He has to pull off three other bunches of buttons to get at the one I asked about—which is when I see what's holding them all in place: one of those extra-big paper clips, bent into sort of an S shape. Clever.

I do a quick count, and there are ten buttons in this bunch, and in the other bunches, too. And instead of stringing each bunch together with thread, Cody used a piece of thin wire.

"How come you put ten buttons in each bunch?"

"The wire is from those twist ties that come on bread and stuff, and ten is about all the buttons you can fit and still have room to twist the wire shut into a loop."

"So who got the idea to use the twist ties and the big paper clips?"

"I don't know—all the guys are doing it. It just happened."

Of course, that's not true. Nothing just happens. But it might already be too late to figure out who did the twisty-clip thing first.

Because it's not like I'm studying some precise experiment in a tidy science lab. This buttons phenomenon has turned into a giant, sloppy, uncontrollable creature that's galloping through the school!

I hand Cody his button bunch, and he clips it back onto a belt loop and walks over to talk with Kevin and Noah. Altogether these guys have at least fifteen button clumps hanging at their waists. As I watch, they pull some off and begin comparing and arguing.

I've got eight minutes before the bell, and I sit down at my desk and open a notebook. I need to record some of my observations while they're still fresh in my mind.

But out of the corner of my eye, I see Brooke come bursting into the room, and she makes a beeline for Ellie and then holds out her hand. So I drop my pencil and hurry over.

Brooke has a beautiful button—it might be the prettiest one I've ever seen. The plastic is sort of a soft, creamy yellowish color, and it's about an inch and a half in diameter—big, but not too big. There are no holes through the button, just one small metal loop on the back. And the best part? Cut into the face of the button there's a pinwheel, with lines that swirl out from the center—at least a dozen—and each groove of the design is stained a rich, dark blue color. The button looks old, but it's not worn or damaged.

The size, the smooth rounded face, the pinwheel design, the strong contrast of the creamy color with the deep blue lines? It's the kind of button that makes you say, *I want it!*

And I know that is *exactly* what Ellie is thinking—even though she's trying not to show it.

Brooke is supposed to believe that Ellie gets to decide what happens next. Because that's how it usually is: Ellie's the boss.

Except who owns that beautiful button? Brooke.

So for the moment, she's in charge, even if she doesn't know it. In a weird kind of way, with that particular button in her hand, Brooke might be the most powerful kid in the room.

In fact . . . that pretty pinwheel button might be more powerful than science itself—even more powerful than common sense. Because at this very moment? I can't help it—I feel like I *have* to get that button!

12

Showdown

I hurry out to my locker in the hall, and I know I'm not being logical, but I don't care. I want that pinwheel button!

From my show-and-tell in social studies that day, I remember how Brooke really loved the specialty buttons, the ones in all the realistic shapes, especially the animals—she wants to become a veterinarian.

So that's the bag I grab from my locker. And it's not like this is going to give away any secrets either. Everyone already knows I have some buttons like this.

Back in the room, Brooke is trying on one of Ellie's ribbon bracelets. I can tell she really likes it.

And Ellie already has the pinwheel button in her hand.

So I might be too late.

Five other girls are watching the action, but from a respectful distance. And usually I'd do the same. Like, whenever we watch a movie together, I always let Ellie pick the one she wants.

But not this time. I move in close, almost between them. And then I say something, just an observation, as if I'm talking about the weather.

"These are those fancy buttons I brought to social studies that day, the ones shaped like dogs and cats and horses and stuff. I've been thinking about how some of these would look on a bracelet."

"*Oooh* . . . that's a *great* idea!"

Brooke is studying my small plastic bag.

And Ellie?

Without even looking, I can tell that her mouth is hanging wide open. She's speechless, but I know that won't last for long.

So I start pulling out buttons. "Yeah, like this kitten . . . and this robin . . . and this pony . . . and this Scottie dog, and then three or four more, maybe on a yellow ribbon? I think that might be really nice—almost like a charm bracelet!"

Brooke is nodding. "So, do you want to trade some of those?"

I say, "Maybe . . . but for what? I mean, these are pretty amazing buttons, and they're almost antiques, too."

Like a cobra, Brooke snatches her pinwheel button right out of Ellie's fingers and hands it to me!

"I'll trade you *that* for *eight* of yours—I get to pick. Deal?"

The word *Deal!* is on my tongue, but before I can say it, Ellie finds her voice.

"*Actually,* Brooke, you and I had already made a trade. You took my bracelet and put it on, and then you handed me that button. So, that's a trade. Plus . . . I was kind of hoping that you'd come for a sleepover this weekend. I got a spool of this *amazing* stretchy cord, and I thought you could help me try out some new ideas for necklaces."

Ellie hasn't even glanced at me. The full power of her smile and her popularity is focused on one thing: poor Brooke. And I can tell Ellie's charm is working, exactly the way it worked on me more times than I can count.

Also, I'm pretty sure that Ellie has never invited Brooke for a sleepover, not until now. So this invitation? It's just a bargaining tool—this is sleepover blackmail!

Which seems totally unfair—a *lot* more unfair than me having all these buttons that Grampa gave me!

But right now the main fact is, *I* have the pinwheel button clamped in my fist. And I am not giving it up.

I look Ellie right in the eye. I keep my voice calm . . . and friendly, too. Which isn't easy. But I'm not using smiles or popularity like she just did—only sharp, cold logic.

"Sorry, Ellie, but if Brooke didn't say 'Deal' to you, then it's pretty clear that she was still *thinking* about trading. And she *did* say 'Deal' to me, and now I'm saying it back: Deal! So, that's that!"

There are seven or eight kids around us now, and they're nodding in agreement. With me.

Before Ellie can say one word, I hand my bag of buttons to Brooke.

"You can take your time picking out the ones you want, okay?"

Brooke gives me sort of a worried smile.

"Um, okay."

If I had known that this was going to be tough on Brooke, I might not have jumped in. And if it hadn't been for Ellie's little sleepover trick, I might have backed away.

But it still feels like I'm doing the right thing here.

I reach over to Brooke's wrist, unhook the red ribbon bracelet, and hold it out to Ellie.

"This is yours."

She glares at me, and the edges of her nostrils are flared out wide—like a horse that's about to kick someone's head off. I've seen this look before, but it's never been aimed at me. I feel like I'm going to shiver, and during that split second I almost hand over Brooke's button and start apologizing.

Almost.

Ellie grabs her bracelet, and as she turns away, the first bell rings.

Walking to my desk, I don't even glance at the pinwheel button—I just slip it into the front pocket of my jeans. And I gulp once or twice.

Because the stuff that just happened? Most of it wasn't about buttons.

13

Ellie's Table

Did I just lose my best friend because of a button?

It's a good question. Also scary.

Sitting in homeroom Friday morning, I don't know the answer.

I mean, I do know how much Ellie hates it when she doesn't get her own way. And *I* just made that happen.

So, does she hate *me* now?

As I keep thinking about this, I have to ask myself a second question, and this one's even scarier: Has Ellie *ever* been my best friend—for real? And what does that even mean?

With a math question, an answer is correct or incorrect, true or false. When I ask, *Is two plus two four?* the answer is, *Yes! Two plus two is four!*

And that's the end of it.

These questions about Ellie and me? I don't see an end.

The best thing about school today is that there's no chance to sit around and make myself unhappy. Mrs. Lang has us doing a combined math and science unit about measurement and averages, and during first-period science, we each get a wooden polygon to measure. Then in fourth-period math, we're going to have to work together and find the average surface area of all of them.

Mrs. Lang has only been a teacher for one year before this one—Dad told me. He checks on things like that. He's a structural engineer, which means he does the math to make sure that buildings and bridges don't fall down. Which is probably part of why he's such a worrier.

The first week or so, I wasn't sure I was going to be able to deal with Mrs. Lang. She was always tense. But I'm starting to understand her. Mostly, I think she's nervous because she's still pretty new at her job. She's got this lesson-planning program on her laptop, and I've seen it open on her desk. She has to describe what she's going to teach in both science and math, and plan out every minute of every class. Mrs. Porter tiptoed into the back of the room one day during math, and then again two days later during science. I can tell Mrs. Lang doesn't like it when the principal comes, so when that happens, I always ask her a hard question. Mrs. Lang is really smart, and when she starts explaining stuff, it's like she forgets that Mrs. Porter is even in the room.

First period goes by fast, and the principal doesn't arrive, and I'm feeling relaxed because Ellie's not here.

It's almost lunch before Brooke gets a chance to give me back my plastic bag. Which is good timing. Because of my trade with her, tons of kids know that I've got a bunch of nice buttons to bargain with. Lunchtime could be good.

And maybe I can talk with Ellie and explain how I went wild about buttons, and sort of apologize.

Hank catches me in the hall outside the cafeteria.

"So . . . did you hear about Ellie's table?"

"What do you mean—what table?"

"Ellie's table, in the cafeteria. She doesn't want you to sit there anymore."

"Oh."

That's all I can think of to say.

I have been right next to Ellie at lunch every school day since my first week of second grade. It never occurred to me that I was sitting at *her* table!

But, of course, what Hank said is true. All that time I thought I was eating lunch with my best friend? I was just a temporary guest.

And Ellie just shredded my invitation.

Hank gives a little cough and shifts from one foot to the other. "Um, we'd better go get in line before they run out of pizza, okay?"

"Right."

As we walk into the cafeteria, I feel a blush creeping

up my neck, and it makes me mad. I've got *nothing* to be embarrassed about, not one thing! But I still feel like kids are watching me, especially from Ellie's table.

And already it seems like the most natural thing in the world to call it that—*Ellie's* table, *Ellie's* table, *Ellie's* table!

But I grab hold of my thinking, and I force it to move off of Ellie. Which is a lot like wrestling.

Then Hank rescues me, just by talking.

"I guess you already figured this out, but I'm really getting into buttons. Which sounds stupid, because half the kids in the whole school are into buttons right now. Except I think it's just a fad with most of them. But I've been doing a lot of research, and I think buttons are almost as interesting as butterflies and moths. And there might be even more different kinds—pretty amazing for something made by humans. Because there are more than a hundred and eighty thousand different species of lepidopterans."

Lepidopterans is the scientific name for butterflies and moths—Hank has already educated me. I mean, I really love science, but he's a superwonk—*if* he gets interested in something. Regular math, and the kind of science study we do in school? He's mostly bored by it. But archaeology? Hank's an expert, especially about the Incas and the Mayas. Mars exploration and how orbits and gravity work? Total geek. Climate change? Seriously nuts on the topic.

And now buttons, or is it buttonology?

I'm reaching for a plate of pizza when someone taps me on the shoulder—a fifth-grade girl I don't know.

"You're Grace, right?"

"Yes. . . ."

"Good, 'cause I heard you've got some great buttons—could I see them?"

"Sure, but first I have to get my lunch."

"Oh, right—sorry. I just didn't want them all to be gone. Because I've got some I want to trade, if you want to. My name is Sarah."

"Well, you can be first in line, I promise."

I mean that as a joke.

But within two minutes after I find a place to sit near the back of the cafeteria, Sarah and three other kids are standing near my table. In a line. Watching me eat.

I've got my bag of buttons on the table, but the pizza tastes great, and I'm not going to rush.

I'm not going to look at Ellie's table either. Not once.

Hank starts poking through the bag. "You know, most of these buttons are celluloid."

"Celluloid?"

"Yeah. It's pretty much the first plastic. And these buttons are old, too—probably from the 1930s or so. They're what button collectors call vintage. This one with the carrot on the yellowish background? It's another kind of early plastic called Bakelite. This *one* button would probably sell on eBay for at least ten dollars, maybe twice that. I got a look at the eight buttons Brooke picked out—probably worth fifteen or twenty dollars, easy."

I pull the pinwheel button out of my pocket. "What about this one?"

"Hmm . . . looks like celluloid—great design, and pretty old, too. Might sell for five or six dollars."

Which means I lost money on my trade with Brooke.

But I don't care. I love my pinwheel.

As I take a drink of milk, I realize something: Hank didn't have to come sit with me. Also, Hank didn't have to tell me all this. He could have offered me trade after trade, picking out the best of my buttons.

Now, Ellie? If *she* knew what Hank knows? She would have snapped up every great button I own, and never thought twice about it! She would have grabbed up all the—

I hit the brakes in my head.

Do I actually *know* what Ellie would have done?

Of course not. And it's bad science to jump to a conclusion like that.

It's also mean.

Still, it's a decent theory. Because that saying "Pretty is as pretty does"? It also works with "friendly."

And Ellie banning me from *her* table?

Not friendly.

I think of all the times I've let Ellie have her own way, never complaining, never letting it bother me. Then I push back just *once,* and BAM—cut off.

So . . . yeah. Hank.

And as I turn to look at him sitting there studying a celluloid button shaped like a fish, suddenly I'm thinking the clearest thought I've thought all day: *Maybe I don't actually need a best friend right now.*

Maybe I just need a better *one.*

14

Halfsies

It's Saturday afternoon, and I'm going on a button hunt with Hank.

Dad likes Hank. They're both into numbers. And also materials—the science of what stuff is made of. My dad has been a Hank fan ever since that day in fourth grade when he started talking about how a strand of spider silk is five times stronger than a strand of steel that's the same thickness, and that Kevlar is stronger than either of them. My dad knew that already, but still, he was impressed. Then Hank began talking about the specific gravity of the three different materials, and the way their molecules link up. And when Hank told him how some butterfly wings get their strength and flexibility from these weird structures called gyroids? That sealed the deal. Hank and Dad became science buddies.

Today's adventure with Hank got started yesterday at lunch when that girl Sarah and three other kids were lined up to see if I wanted to trade any of my fancy buttons. I told Hank how I was looking to get some larger buttons, and that they didn't have to be special like the pinwheel—just big, and sort of interesting.

So Hank became my button-trading advisor.

I left the cafeteria with four more large buttons: three made of celluloid, and a dark green beauty with carvings on it made of Bakelite. Because of Hank, I only had to trade away five of my smaller specialty buttons.

Out in the hallway, just before I headed for math and Hank went toward the gym, he said, "I've got an idea about where we might find some good buttons to collect, or to trade—whichever. Interested?"

My favorite thing about what Hank said? He used the word *we*—one of the friendliest words ever.

Of course, I *was* interested, and Hank told me his idea, and I liked it.

And that's why I'm climbing into the back seat of his mom's car.

"Hi, Hank—hi, Mrs. Powell."

"Hi, Grace. I don't think I've seen you since the open house at school last October. You've gotten taller!"

I never know how to answer when grown-ups say stuff like that.

Hank looks sideways at his mom.

"Kind of an obvious thing to say, Mom. It's been almost a year—Grace wouldn't be *shrinking*, would she?"

"Just making friendly conversation, Henry."

"It's *Hank*."

Mrs. Powell backs the car out of our driveway, and as she starts forward, her eyes find me in the rearview mirror.

"Hank says that you're the one who started this buttons fad at school. And he told us about the other things you found at that old textile mill in Maine."

"It was in Massachusetts, Mom."

"Sorry—Massachusetts. Did you ever imagine kids would get so interested in buttons? Because *some* people find them absolutely fascinating!"

"Very funny, Mom."

Hank turns so he can see me from the front seat. "So, you brought some money?"

"Fifteen dollars. How about you?"

"About the same. That ought to be enough, except there's no guarantee that we can find any buttons for sale. I hunted around online for places that run estate sales for families—which is how I found the three shops we're going to try first."

Mrs. Powell takes a quick look at Hank.

"*Three* shops? I thought we were going to *one* store in Sheridan Grove—which is already a twenty-minute drive, practically in Wisconsin! Why don't we just go to a nice antiques shop, maybe in Clifton Woods?"

"Because the people who run antiques shops charge high prices. We're looking for a bargain, so we're going to thrift shops. And Sheridan Grove is nowhere near Wisconsin."

The drive is more like forty minutes, and Mrs. Powell is not happy, especially when we arrive at the address Hank gave her.

"Carrie's Thrift Barn? This place looks pretty run-down!"

"It'll be fine, Mom. C'mon, Grace, let's go." And he opens the car door.

"Wait—you are *not* going in there by yourselves!"

"Fine. But let us go first, and when you come in, keep away from us, okay?"

The look on her face? Her feelings are hurt, and right away Hank says, "Sorry, that sounded bad. All I mean is, you look like you've got plenty of money because you *do,* and people who look that way don't get bargains at places like this."

She stares at Hank. "How do you *know* things like that?"

"Research."

I've been to tons of garage sales with my mom, but this is my first time ever inside a thrift store. It's a big place with a low ceiling, and there are three or four women, some alone and some with kids, walking up and down the long aisles, picking things off racks, putting them back, and sometimes holding shirts or coats or dresses up against their kids to see what might fit. I spot a couple of guys, too. A lot of the clothes are really nice. Even Ellie would like some of the tops and skirts I look at. And then it strikes me—some of these might have actually *been* Ellie's, before she got tired of them and jetted over to London or Paris for all *new* ones.

But that's a mean thought, and I shove it away. Ellie is *not* going to poison my Saturday.

The front door chimes, and Hank's mom walks in and starts wandering around, trying to avoid us. Hank was right. His mom does *not* look like the other shoppers here.

"Over there," Hank says. And he points at a hand-lettered sign hanging on a string from the ceiling: ESTATE SALES—NEW ARRIVALS.

The stuff below the sign is mostly still in cardboard moving boxes, and a lot of them have been written on with markers—labels like *family room, downstairs bedroom,* and *basement.* The boxes are spread around on the floor, with the flaps open and the contents jumbled. I know that I'm looking at leftovers from the lives of other people, other families, and I can't help feeling a little sad.

Not Hank. His mind is like a laser beam.

"You check through that bunch over there, and I'll start right here with this group, okay?"

"Got it."

Kitchen utensils, board games, puzzles, toys, clothes, plates and bowls and glasses, purses, hand tools, shoes and boots, sheets and towels—so much stuff. And looking for buttons feels like hunting for a quarter on a soccer field. Which is something I've done before. Unsuccessfully.

But I begin to see a pattern, see the way this house was organized. There were two bathrooms, probably one up-stairs and one downstairs, because there are two boxes of bathroomy stuff. And there was definitely a family room because four boxes have that label—duh. And I keep trying to think, if this were *my* house, and I had some sewing stuff, where would I keep it? And as I'm thinking this, out in the middle of eight or ten boxes, I spot a flap with the label *downstairs hall closet*. I have to kind of wade out to it, trying not to step inside any boxes. And once I'm there, I know I'm getting warmer. The downstairs hall closet was definitely the catchall at this house, the place to stick whatever doesn't quite belong anywhere else. At our house, there's a drawer in the kitchen like that. And also the utility closet in the laundry room. Plus half the basement.

There are actually *three* boxes of stuff from this same closet. And in the second one, I find a basket, and it's the sewing stuff. But it's not a big basket, only about six inches across and four inches deep.

And down on the bottom, I see some buttons, maybe twenty, mostly small and mostly white.

Dead end.

There are several bundles of folded fabric in the box, and some of the cloth is so old that it's sort of yellowed, almost brittle. But I spot a deep blue fabric with yellow ducks printed on it, and when I lift it out to get a better look, underneath it there's a large round cookie tin with a snowy winter scene on the lid. And written on the top with a green marker? One word: *buttons*.

About an hour later we're back at Hank's house in the basement playroom with at least two thousand buttons spread out across a Ping-Pong table. We only went to that one thrift shop after all, which made his mom happy. And for now we've got *plenty* of new buttons to mess with.

Hank says, "First I think we should sort them all by what they're made of, okay?"

"Sure—that makes sense."

I can tell Hank really wants to be in charge of the sorting process, which is fine by me. He sticks pieces of masking tape at different places on the table and then starts writing on each one with a Sharpie.

"Okay, so celluloid buttons go here . . . then Bakelite . . . Lucite . . . vegetable ivory . . . china—"

"'Vegetable ivory'? What's *that*?"

"It's an ivory substitute made from the nut of the tagua palm tree, which grows in the tropics."

"Oh. And Lucite?"

"That's a kind of clear, hard plastic. Yeah, so, china . . . glass . . . mother-of-pearl . . . leather . . . bone . . . and wood."

"You don't mean, like, actual *bone*?"

"Yeah—sometimes antlers were used, but mostly cow bones."

He scans the whole batch of buttons and reaches out and picks one up. "Wow! I didn't think we'd have *any* of these, but check it out! This is bone."

He's got a button about the size of a dime on his palm,

sort of a pale yellowish color, and there are two large holes, like the eyes on a happy face.

"This was probably made by hand, maybe as far back as 1850. See how the holes are uneven? That's how you can tell this one wasn't made on a machine. And if you looked at it through a strong magnifying lens, you could see the lines in the bone where the blood used to flow— not smooth like plastic."

That kind of grosses me out. But the science is interesting. Buttons made of cow bones—who knew?

Hank Powell, that's who.

The sorting goes pretty fast once I learn what to look for, and Hank's a good teacher. In no time at all, I can tell the difference between vegetable ivory and Bakelite with my eyes shut. Almost.

Also, when Hank doesn't know something, he doesn't pretend he does. And I like that. As we sort, he keeps stopping to search on the internet, to be sure he's not messing up.

After the sorting comes the dividing.

Hank says, "So . . . do you want to pick first, or should I?"

I can tell he's nervous about this part. Our deal from the start was simple—whatever we find, we go halfsies.

So I smile and say, "You should go first."

Because I've already decided that Hank can have whichever buttons he wants. He's the one who's getting into collecting them, plus he thought up this whole plan. And it's not like I need any more buttons. At all. Ever.

We take turns choosing from each group, one material after the other. I pick just enough of the nicer buttons of each kind so that Hank doesn't feel like I don't care. Because I know he wouldn't like that.

Seeing his face get all lit up about a *button*? It's great.

And it's sweet, too, because he tries to make me take some of the ones that I can tell he's dying to keep.

"Are you sure you don't want this burgundy-and-ivory octagon? I mean, it's a classic two-tone Bakelite, and look at the carving, and the edges—they're so *crisp*!"

"Thanks, but I like the lighter colors."

So sweet!

An alarm bell goes off in my head.

Because *sweet* is a word I don't use much, and I just used it twice in the past thirty seconds.

So I take a careful look at Hank as he's trying to decide which mother-of-pearl buttons to choose first.

I like what I see—I do. He's cute . . . in a tallish, thin-nish, awkwardish sort of way. Dark hair and eyes, straight nose, a mouth that smiles a lot. It's all nice. But mostly Hank looks . . . smart. And that's mainly in his eyes, the way he's always got a question there.

I think he likes the way I look, too. But I know that's not the reason why we're friends.

We go back and forth, dividing up the pearly buttons, and then the glass, the china, the leather, the celluloid, and the bone.

There are only five of the bone buttons, and I make

Hank take them all. For his collection. And then he says I should get to keep the old container the buttons came in, because I'm the one who found it.

Halfsies.

After we're done, my mom comes and picks me up. And riding home with a cookie tin of buttons on my lap, I think about the afternoon.

I also think about Ellie.

On a regular Saturday during the school year, I'd have spent at least a couple of hours with her. She'd have called and said something like, *I'm going to go get some shoes—want to come?* or, *I feel like seeing that new movie—want to come?* Because time with Ellie is mostly me tagging along while she does whatever she wants to.

Still, I sort of miss that.

But today was good. It was me, Hank, and a bunch of buttons: three different elements mixed together.

When elements combine, they don't actually change, but they sometimes link up and form a new compound, the way hydrogen and oxygen join to make water.

That's how this feels.

And if I had to describe this new compound?

It's 99 percent fun and 1 percent sweet.

15

Long Distance

Grandpa

Sunday 7:47 PM

You there Grampa?

Yup. How are you?

Good. You?

All good here. Picked the last of the tomatoes all afternoon. Sitting down now—feels great.

So I've got a question. About buttons.

What a surprise! : >) Shoot.

Do you think Gramma kept any buttons around the house? You still have some of her stuff, right?

Grampa?

Sorry. Yes, I still have all her things. Maybe in her upstairs sitting room? Haven't been in there for quite some time.

Oh. Well never mind. I've got PLENTY of buttons! I took a picture last week of the ones we have here in our house, and then yesterday I went with this boy named Hank to a thrift shop and we found a huge tin of buttons all from one family over a long time. So I'm kind of interested in comparing. Here's a pic I took of our Hamlin family buttons:

And here's the bunch from the thrift store:

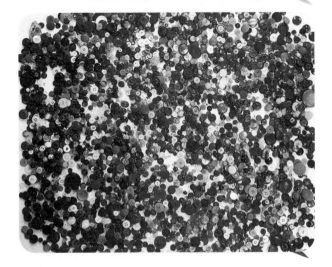

Interesting, huh?

Very. Sort of like little graveyards. When a button drops off, you pop it into the graveyard.

That's way too gloomy Grampa. But yeah, I get that. Still, I'd just call each group a collection.

Collection, final resting place, graveyard—pretty much all the same. Just being accurate, Gracie.

But mostly gloomy and sad . . . I can hear your voice when we text—you know that, right? Maybe let's call them . . . time capsules.

I like that. A family buttons time capsule.

Yes—much nicer.

This Hank fellow—would I approve?

Definitely. Even Dad likes him.

That's quite impressive!
Details, if you don't mind . . .

You remember Ellie, right?

Of course—the unforgettable Miss Emerson.

Well we're not best friends anymore. Or even friends at all. And Hank used to be on her *approved* list, but then he totally ditched her and stuck with me instead. That's about all there is to it.

I like him already.

He's really smart—collects butterflies and moths. And now buttons. Diving deep.

Fourteen monarch butterflies passed through our garden three days after you left, going to Mexico—and it'll take them two or three generations to even get there. Always so amazing. Your grandmother planted those four purple butterfly bushes along the garden fence—remember? The monarchs and the swallowtails can't resist the blooms. Such a treat, even now.

I hear your voice again Grampa. Sorry you still miss her so much. Me too.

Yes, you too. I'm glad my neighbors don't live close, because they'd hear me talking to her now and then. And the way you hear my voice when we text? I can hear hers too. And guess what? She tells me the same things you do—stop being sad, keep being grateful. And that self-pity nonsense? KNOCK IT OFF!

Haha—I can hear her saying that too!

But things are better. That old mill building is just what I need right now. I've got my first big meetings with contractors coming up this week. And I can't wait to send you the specs for the solar panels I'm installing on the roof—wonderful progress. And not as much time to be sad!

I'm so glad—I love that place! You know what the building was like before you got hold of it?

What?

A graveyard!

Haha—good one! You got me back! How about your week? Big stuff coming there? Projects, reports, holding hands with Hank?

Soooo *funny* Grampa. No, nothing much coming this week. Except this buttons thing? It turned into this huge fad at school, totally goofy. And I have no idea where it's all going.

Wherever it goes, I have this hunch that you'll be right in the middle of it. Take good notes, and keep me in the loop! Is your giant cache of buttons still a secret?

You, me, Mom, Dad, Ben. That's it.

I won't tell a soul!

Good. I love you Grampa.

I love you too Gracie. Have a happy night.

And you take good notes too, and keep me in the loop about our mill building okay?

Will do—I promise! Good night.

Nite.

16

Easier

"**Y**ou're kind of quiet this morning."

"Just thinking."

I can tell that Mom wants me to talk more, but I know she's not going to push it. She's good with silence.

And anyway, if I talked to her? I don't think she'd like what I have to say. I'm still kind of stuck on graveyards—ever since I texted with Grampa last night. He was so sad about Gramma.

When I asked Mom if she would drive me this morning, she said, *Sure*—no questions asked. I wanted to avoid the scene on the bus. I feel like gangs of button maniacs would pounce on me, looking for trades.

Of course, I don't actually know if buttons are even still a thing.

Maybe over the weekend everybody decided buttons are dumb. Maybe there's some new fad I don't know about, some online craze that lit up the screens, blasting the buttons out of every single kid's head.

Right back into all the little button graveyards.

"So, where do you think Gramma is right now?"

Mom smiles a little, her eyes on the traffic. But it's like my question doesn't surprise her one bit.

"I don't know, Grace—not for sure. If you're asking me if your grandmother is still herself, still *somewhere*, then I would say yes, I believe she is. But do I *know* that, the same way I know that the sun comes up every morning? Then, no, I don't know it like that."

"Then how come you believe she's still herself? Are you saying that you think Gramma's still alive but somewhere else—like heaven?"

We're backed up at a stoplight now, moving ahead only a little with each green signal. And Mom is thinking before she answers me.

"I don't recall if I've ever told you this before. I was about twenty years old, and in one of my college courses, the professor asked the whole class to close our eyes and sit very still. Then she asked, 'Is it possible for you to imagine that the world you've known your whole life isn't there anymore?' And I decided I could imagine that, no problem. Then she said, 'Is it possible for you to imagine that your physical body is not sitting in a chair in some classroom, that your body isn't really anywhere in this world at all?' And again, that was pretty easy for me to imagine. Then she asked, 'Is it possible for you to imagine that the part of you that is doing all this imagining could just stop it, and never think anything at all, ever again?'

And after about a minute of sitting there thinking, I decided I could *not* imagine that—not at all."

"Those are some weird questions!"

"I agree. It turned out that our professor was borrowing them from a philosopher named Descartes, and we went on to study a lot of his writings. But I never forgot that moment. And I believe that Gramma is still herself, still thinking, still loving you and Ben and your dad and me and Grampa."

"So . . . you're saying people don't really die when they die?"

"I'm saying that I think I can see how that would be possible. Do I *know* it, for sure? No. And I guess I won't completely know any of this for sure until that moment when *I* die, or rather, when I *don't* die—when I figure out that I haven't stopped thinking or stopped being myself. Where I will be at that moment, or what any of that will be like—I have no idea. Not yet."

"So this is a theory."

"Correct. A theory."

I'm quiet, and the traffic starts moving again.

Mom reaches over and pats my arm. "Pretty deep thoughts for a sunny Monday morning."

"Yeah . . . sorry."

"Don't apologize. I love the way you think and think and think—always have, always will."

"Thanks."

We have another quiet stretch before her next question.

"Did I hear you tell Dad that you and Ellie are having some troubles?"

"Uh-huh—at least right now."

"Sorry to hear that. You two have been friends for a long time."

"Yeah."

I don't say more because I don't know if there's anything else to say. But I do think of a question. "Of all the kids you knew back when you were in sixth grade, are any of them still your friends?"

"No, not a single one. My family moved from Ohio to Massachusetts, then from Massachusetts to Illinois, and then back to a different town in Massachusetts, all before I graduated from high school. It's hard to keep in touch with school friends. I know I could track down some of them now if I wanted to, but once you lose contact, there are fewer reasons to pick up the threads again. And I was out of high school before Facebook and texting and all that came along. Now it's a lot easier."

"Yeah, totally."

Easier.

Easier is a very nice idea.

There are about a hundred things that I wish would get easier, right now, right this second.

Except wishing isn't scientific.

"Isn't that Hank Powell, standing there near the door?"

We're pulling into the drop-off area in front of the school, and Mom's right.

"That's him."

"Say hello to him for me, will you?"

"Sure."

"And have a wonderful day, Grace. You know how you're always telling your father to stop worrying? Take your own advice, okay?"

"Okay. Thanks for the ride."

"You're welcome—I love you, Grace."

"I love you, too. Bye."

"Bye."

As the car pulls away, Hank sees me and waves, a smile on his face.

I smile back, partly just to be friendly. But there's another reason for my smile: I can see that walking into the school this morning is going to be better than I thought it would be.

It's going to be easier.

17

The Catalyst

"**I** made six *fantastic* trades on the bus!"

These are Hank's first words of the new week—not *Hi,* not *Great to see you,* not *How are you?* So I guess the buttons thing is still going strong, at least for him. I've never seen Hank so totally hyper.

"On Friday? I saw some guys who had made these bunches of buttons with little twist ties, so I made myself twenty of them using some of the junky buttons we found on Saturday, duplicates and stuff."

"Yeah, I noticed those kids, too."

"So anyway, this morning I was looking for anything special in the bunches they had—sometimes just one button out of a whole set. And if I spotted a good one, then I would offer to trade *two* bunches for one bunch—just to get that *particular* button. And it worked like magic! But the best part? After I take the one button I want from a bunch, then I *add* an extra button to fill it back up, and just like that, I've got *another* bunch of ten to trade with! Pretty great, huh?"

I nod, but I'm also doing math in my head—because what Hank just described makes a really neat equation: Twenty bunches minus the two bunches he trades leaves eighteen, but then he *adds* one bunch back—which makes nineteen; minus the next two bunches leaves seventeen, but then he *adds* one back, to make eighteen, and so on— all the way down to one last single bunch left. There's a special name for that kind of math progression . . . maybe recursive?

Hank says, "Right now I've still got *fourteen* bunches left, and I've already made *six* trades, and three of my new buttons are *amazing*! I'm going to be able to trade two bunches for one bunch *nineteen* times! Isn't that *great*?"

"It is! Really smart!"

Hank's got me grinning now—I can't help it. Ben went nuts about his new clarinet, and Grampa was excited about the old mill, but Hank is almost exploding!

He takes a deep breath, and he looks embarrassed. I hope there wasn't some weird look on my face just now to make him feel that way.

He calms himself down, almost serious. "But I'm going to have to cool it till after homeroom. Mr. Scott has a new rule: no buttons in his room. So remember that before you go to language arts. What about you? Got any button plans for today?"

"Not really, but I'll keep my eyes open."

That's what I say, but the truth is that I'm just not into the buttons thing today.

But I'm very curious to see what's up with the fad. And I promised Grampa I'd take good notes!

We head toward the sixth-grade hall, and the first thing I notice is that those boys don't have any button bunches hooked onto their belts today. The bunches are on short loops of cord now. Which makes sense. All those clumps hanging everywhere? Way too awkward.

I also spot five different groups of second- and third-grade kids along the corridor, comparing handfuls of buttons and trading . . . which means button fever is spreading to the younger grades.

"Your little sister—what grade is she in now?"

A groan from Hank. "Third. I finally convinced my mom that I *had* to have a lock on my door. Hannah is driving me nuts."

"Has she claimed some of the family buttons so she can bring them to school? Is she into collecting like you are?"

"No way—not interested. She's more of a mad-scientist type. Last week she pulled the heads and the arms and the legs off five of her dolls so she could switch them all around onto the different bodies. My mom got pretty freaked out, but I told her not to worry. It's actually a smart way to mix up a boring doll collection—now she's got five new little Frankenstein dolls!"

That gets me laughing, and then I try to recall if Ellie ever made me laugh like this—yes . . . only not as often.

Do I want to compare Hank with Ellie? No.

But it keeps happening.

Which makes me wish I could stop observing my own thinking. Which only makes me think more.

Hank's been thinking, too.

"How many different kinds of button kids can we identify? So far, I've only seen one actual collector—me. I'm calling myself a hunter-gatherer. Then there are kids like that guy."

He points at a boy swinging a shoelace loop that must be loaded with forty or fifty bunches of buttons. "I'd call him a getter—someone who just wants *more*."

"How about traders, kids who like making the deals more than they like the buttons themselves?"

Hank nods. "Absolutely—traders are a definite species."

"And I've also spotted three or four color nuts, kids who mostly go after one particular color."

He smiles. "And then there are the metalheads."

"Right, and the military metalheads are a subspecies." Then, trying not to sound too curious, I say, "How about Ellie? What's her category?"

"Hmm . . . maybe a crafter? On account of the stuff she's making? But . . . when Ellie got us all to bring buttons to lunch? That's what really got things moving. And then the first bracelet she made last week? That got a *ton* of kids hooked. Might have to call Ellie a trendsetter. Which means a lot of the other kids are followers."

I'm a little scared to ask this, but I say it anyway. "So . . . what would you call me?"

"You?"

He has to pause, and I'm worried that I've put him on the spot, that he thinks I'm trying to be cute, or that I'm only—

"I've got it—you're the *catalyst*! Except that's not a category, because there's only *one* catalyst. You started everything. And when you gave away those buttons last week after lunch? That was *pivotal*! Without you, none of this would be happening. I wouldn't be collecting, and I wouldn't know what Bakelite is or how it got used to make fantastic Art Deco buttons—I wouldn't even know what Art Deco *means*!"

Catalyst.

I like that.

I like it so much I almost blush.

It's a word I know from chemistry. A catalyst releases energy. Add the right catalyst, and a process speeds up— like a solid turning to a liquid, or a liquid separating into different gases.

Of course, a catalyst can also make everything burst into flames and destroy the whole lab.

So, yeah . . . Grace the Catalyst.

We stop beside the art room bulletin boards because Hank has to turn here to head for Mr. Scott's homeroom. I think he wants to say something, so I wait.

And I'm right.

"See you at lunch, okay?"

"Okay."

"And listen—don't let Ellie bug you today. She thinks

she runs everything, but she doesn't. You're ten times smarter than she's ever been. Ten times nicer, too."

He says the last bit with half a smile.

"Thanks." And I smile back.

Then Hank walks his way, and I walk mine.

So . . . did my face tell Hank that I needed cheering up?

Because I really did. And what he just said worked: I feel better.

But as I get closer to Mrs. Lang's room, the feeling evaporates.

I'm not ready for today—not ready to deal with Ellie, not ready for the whole button circus. I wish it would all go away.

I don't even care anymore that wishing isn't scientific.

Still, unless I totally chicken out and run for the nurse's office, I know I'm stuck. Because the one sure thing about a school day? Once it starts, it just keeps going.

And mine begins with homeroom. Right now.

18

Only a Button

I shouldn't have been worried about Ellie. She's way too busy to care about me.

Her button jewelry has its own brand name now: Ellie's Originals. She's got a sign on a desk just inside Mrs. Lang's doorway so that girls from up and down our hall can stop in and trade away all their very best buttons for necklaces and anklets and, of course, her newest bracelets.

I wonder . . . *Is Ellie also selling raffle tickets for sleepovers at her house?*

Which is a mean thought.

But that's definitely something Ellie would do—only she's not smart enough to think of it.

Which is an even meaner thought.

I walk into the room, slipping right past her.

Two minutes later, then three, and she's still busy, only aware of her customers.

Although . . . Ellie might just be *pretending* not to notice me.

Because that's what I'm doing. I keep sneaking quick looks at her, and maybe she's doing that, too.

Or maybe not.

Either way, if I can get through homeroom with zero contact, that'll suit me fine. Then I won't have to see her until social studies.

Mrs. Lang must have noticed all this button craziness—how could she not? But her eyes are glued to the screen of her laptop, and she's tapping away at her lesson plans as if she expects ten visits from the principal today.

Over at the windows I've got a good view of the black-top beside the building, and the bell hasn't rung yet for the third, fourth, and fifth graders. A bunch of fourth-grade boys are playing a game where they each stand at a line and toss a button at a target drawn on the asphalt with chalk. The kid who gets a button to land closest to the center gets to keep the other ones. All over the playground, kids are standing in small groups, passing buttons around, looking at them, flipping them back and forth, making trades. And the button kids way outnumber the others who are running around or tossing balls or using the swings and slides.

Buttons! I still can't get my head around this thing! Just last Wednesday eight kids brought some buttons to lunch. At Ellie's table.

That was only five days ago! And now it's a full-on fad. Is that even possible, in only five days?

The fact is, it's *more* than possible, because I'm looking at the proof right there on the playground—and here in my own homeroom. This is happening!

"Hi, Grace."

"Oh—hi, Brooke. How's it going?"

"Okay."

"So, did you have that sleepover at Ellie's?"

I'm half joking, but Brooke doesn't pick up on it. She shakes her head, then glances toward the doorway.

"Ellie's not talking to me, not even looking at me."

"Yeah, I guess we're both pretty much invisible today!"

She doesn't smile at all.

I shouldn't keep trying to joke about this. Not with Brooke.

"Ellie had Taylor for a sleepover on Saturday. I guess I really made her mad. But like you said, I hadn't agreed to a deal yet—I *hadn't*!"

"Well, I'm really sorry I jumped into the middle of things. I guess I went too far trying to get that pinwheel."

"It's okay. I mean, it was only a button, right? And if someone wants to get all upset and mean about it, then that's not my fault. Right?"

"Right."

But Brooke thinks it *is* her fault. Which is exactly the way Ellie wants her to feel.

Ellie is at the center of her own imaginary solar system, and Brooke and me? We're both in some cold, dark corner behind a lost moon, and we've each got a big label glued onto our foreheads:

Ellie's Not My Friend Anymore and
It's All My Fault!

But actually . . . if this situation is anybody's fault, it's *my* fault.

If I hadn't barged in to get that button, we'd all still be friends . . . or at least we'd be talking to each other the way we always did before.

And eating lunch together. At Ellie's table.

Which wasn't so bad—in fact, it was mostly good.

I guess.

And Brooke? She's completely innocent. She didn't deserve to get pulled into my collision with Ellie. It's like I caused a black hole to open up, and now the gravity has a grip on everybody.

"Here." I reach into my pocket and hand her the pinwheel button. "You should go and see if Ellie still wants to trade you for a bracelet or something. So you can fix things with her."

"But . . . this is yours now."

"I know, but like you said, it's only a button. And this'll make me feel a lot better about everything."

A smile makes Brooke look like a whole different person.

"This is so nice, Grace—thanks!"

"You're welcome."

I try not to watch, but Brooke goes and waits her turn at Ellie's store. Then they talk, and there's an exchange, and Ellie stands up and gives Brooke a little hug.

I go back to watching the third and fourth graders swapping and flipping and tossing buttons around outside.

And I really do feel better.

The good feeling lasts all day. I see Ellie during social studies, then at lunch, gym, and language arts. We don't talk, but it seems like she almost smiles at me a few times.

Five minutes before the bell at the end of the day, Brooke stops at my desk in homeroom. And she's wearing her new bracelet—a dark blue ribbon with white buttons.

"Ellie wanted me to give you this. See you tomorrow, and thanks again!"

It's a piece of paper folded sort of like an envelope, and there's a note on the outside, written in Ellie's perfect cursive:

Brooke told me what you did,
so I wanted you to have this.

And when I unfold the paper, it's the pinwheel button! Except . . . not quite.

It's been snapped into three jagged pieces, totally destroyed.

19

Scars

I'm not getting mad, I'm not getting mad, I'm not getting mad! It's just a stupid button—let it go!

It *was* just a stupid button, and this morning I knew that—that's why it was so easy to give it to Brooke, to let it go. I wanted to get our universe back into balance.

But *now*? Now this button stands for every unkind thing that Ellie's ever done—things I went along with, things I didn't even think about.

Because it's not like Ellie turned mean all of a sudden. Little bits of meanness have been around for a long time, just not so much out in the open.

Before, I used to laugh when Ellie whispered something about another girl, about how awful her clothes looked, or how someone's nose was shaped funny, or how some girl talked too loud or said something dumb.

And now the meanness is aimed at me.

So I probably deserve this.

What did I like about Ellie, anyway? How come I thought we were such great friends?

That's a hard question.

Then it hits me: Other kids must have thought *I* was kind of mean, too, because I was Ellie's friend!

Did some of her meanness rub off on me, just from hanging out every day? Did I get infected—is that how meanness spreads . . . scientifically?

And how mean did I let myself get? Did I go along with Ellie so we could keep being friends?

I guess I must have.

But I know it's not really accurate to think about Ellie as if she were this totally horrible person. I've seen her good side, too—I have. She can be generous, sort of. And kind, sort of. And also clever, and silly, and even sweet . . . truly sweet.

Like when she got choked up talking about the buttons that had been on her grandfather's suits? That was *totally* sweet!

So maybe I need to find the *least* mean way to deal with this . . . incident.

Maybe I need to keep trying to be kind to Ellie, no matter what.

Or maybe even just let it go, let it drift away into space, let it vanish without reacting at all.

I'm still sitting at my desk as the final bell rings, and I notice that my right hand is throbbing. So I look down, and it hurts to open my fist.

I've been squeezing the broken pinwheel button with so much force that the rough edges have pressed little red dents and ridges deep into the skin of my palm.

Like scars.

When water reaches its freezing point, it turns to ice instantly. And just like that, I feel a decision snap into place—clear and cold and hard.

I am *not* letting Ellie get away with this!

20

Fad Gone Bad

"**S**o . . . I heard you'll trade eight of these for one bracelet. Is that true?"

It's Audrey Harken. She's in Mrs. Casey's homeroom, and she's looking through my bag of fancy buttons.

"That's right, and you can pick whichever ones you want."

"*Nice*—here you go!"

She slaps a bracelet down on the lunch table and begins choosing.

I've still got at least a hundred of the specialty buttons here at school—which is good, because they're very popular. But I've also got six other bags of nice vintage buttons in reserve—the same ones that I had planned to dump onto a tray last week at Ellie's lunchtime button show.

As Audrey leaves, I say, "Be sure to tell the kids in your homeroom that I'm looking for bracelets and necklaces, and I've got *lots* of really great buttons here!"

My new business is bouncing along nicely on this fine Tuesday morning, and everybody loves my sign: GRACE'S GORGEOUS GOODIES. So far, I've traded for nine bracelets, three necklaces, and one anklet—all made by Ellie. And I've still got fifteen minutes before lunch is over. If all goes well, by the end of the day most of Ellie's Originals are going to belong to one person: *me.*

Hank's been watching since lunch period began, and I can feel his eyes, feel his questions. I feel some disapproval, too. And it's not because I'm getting rid of so many great old buttons—I already let him pick through my stuff and choose all the ones he wanted, for free. For his collection.

So that's not what he disapproves of.

No, Hank can tell something else is going on here. I haven't shown him the broken pinwheel button, but he can see that what I'm doing has an edge to it—something a little sharp, a little harsh, a little grim.

And he's right.

Because this isn't about fun with buttons. This is war. Grace's Gorgeous Goodies and Ellie's Originals are locked in a desperate battle to the death.

Okay—that's too dramatic.

But no matter what this is called, so far I'm *winning.*

And it feels wonderful.

I've seen Ellie look this way a few times from over there at her own special lunch table, trying to figure out what I'm doing. But she's too stuck-up to walk over and take a look. And she's probably not smart enough to send a spy, which is what I'd do.

Besides, it doesn't matter if she knows what I'm doing. She can't stop me, because when it comes to buttons, I'm probably the richest kid in the world!

And here comes another customer—Brooke.

"I like your sign! So, what kind of goodies have you got here?"

"Oh, you know—you've seen a lot of these already."

She picks up the same bag of fancy buttons that she looked through last Friday, when I got her to trade me for that pinwheel.

"I *love* this seahorse! And another one, a perfect pair! I can't believe I didn't see these! Want to trade something for them?"

"Actually, *I* love that bracelet you've got. So, how about taking both seahorses, plus any other six buttons you want. For the bracelet."

"I don't know. . . . This is a great bracelet."

"It really is. You should probably hang on to it."

"Yeah."

And honestly, I don't want Brooke to get involved again.

But she's still poking around in the buttons bag. "*Oooh*—check out this one—looks like a bluebird. Do you know why this one's transparent, but the seahorses aren't?"

"Hank could tell you."

Hank looks up from his cup of fruit salad, and Brooke takes the button to him at the far end of the table.

"The bird is celluloid. That's why the color is so bright, but the plastic still lets the light through. And this button is vintage—probably at least seventy years old. The seahorses were carved out of Bakelite, which is much denser. They're vintage, too."

It's a thorough answer, but he's not happy that I pulled him into my business. Because Brooke's cute blue ribbon bracelet with the small white buttons? It's almost *mine*. And Hank knows it, and he wants no part of what I'm doing.

Brooke is back standing beside me, and I make her an offer.

"How about this: You can take the two seahorses, the bluebird, plus *seven* other buttons—ten great buttons for that bracelet. Because it's such a good one."

"Um . . . I think that's fair. Okay, it's a deal!"

And just like that, I've got another one of Ellie's Originals.

As Brooke walks away, Hank is getting ready to go dump his lunch tray. But instead of standing up, he slides down toward my end of the table.

"I've never seen you wearing bracelets or jewelry, and it's not like Ellie's been using anything rare or fancy to make her stuff. So, how come you're collecting it?"

"Simple. Because when Ellie figures out that I've got all these, she's going to *hate* it. And there's not one thing she can do about it. I'm going to teach her a lesson."

"So . . . this is payback for getting dumped from her lunch table?"

"That's part of it."

"What's the rest?"

"It's complicated. It would take all day to explain."

Hank gives me a look. "I figured out how gravitational orbits work. Do you think it's more complicated than *that*?"

"Actually, yes. Figuring out what's going on between Ellie and me isn't the same as working math problems. If it *were* the same, all the wars in the world could be ended in a week!"

"So . . . when does *this* war end?"

I shrug. "When *I've* won, and when Ellie—"

"Hands OFF!"

I turn to look just as Kevin shoves Cody. They're two tables away, and they each have a lunch tray covered with buttons.

"That one's *mine,* and you know it!"

Cody jumps to his feet and shoves Kevin back, then makes a grab for something on Kevin's tray, but he misses. Both trays fly off the far side of the table, and hundreds of buttons go bouncing across the tile floor.

"Kevin! Cody! Stop it!"

Mrs. Casey and the custodian are headed their way, but Kevin stands up and gets both arms around Cody, and they wrestle each other to the floor. As Mrs. Casey and Mr. Roberts pull them apart, kids are yelling and squabbling and chasing the spilled buttons all over the cafeteria. It's like a riot, and it started in three seconds!

Hank looks at the chaos around us, then at me.

"When I did a report on the Klondike Gold Rush last year, I read about how the prospectors and miners began fighting with each other. Looks like the Great Button Rush might be turning ugly. And *your* little war isn't so nice either."

Then he takes his tray and leaves.

I hate being scolded, especially when I deserve it.

Because Hank's right—I'm out for revenge here, and it's not pretty.

I'm glad I didn't get to finish telling him the rest of my plan, because Ellie's going to get every one of her "Originals" back—ripped up into tiny, ragged pieces.

Hank would have been shocked to hear me say that.

Maybe even disgusted.

Except, I don't care. I'm being illogical, and I'm being unscientific—and I know that, and I understand that, and I accept that.

Why? Because Ellie Emerson totally needs something she has never had—not once in her whole mean, spoiled, selfish life: She needs a crushing defeat.

And that's what she's going to get. From me.

A question starts to bubble up in my mind.

I try to push it away, but the words arrive anyway, and I can't ignore them:

If I'm doing such a great job winning my war with Ellie, then how come I feel so awful?

21

Kitchen Time

Ben drops his backpack onto a chair and stands there, looking at the kitchen table. And then at me.

"What's up with the festival of weird foods?"

"Nothing. And mind your own business."

Ben studies the wreckage in front of me.

"A peach yogurt, a box of Thin Mints, a full roll of Ritz crackers, half a block of cheddar cheese, and two little cans of tomato juice. And you snarfed all that in about fifteen minutes. So, yeah, I can see that everything must be totally fine."

"Mind your own business!"

He goes to the fridge. "Hey—one yogurt left!"

He sits down across the table from me, peels back the foil cover, and begins eating. He's using a huge spoon and making the most horrible sounds he can. On purpose.

"Stop being disgusting."

"You ate *that,* and *I'm* disgusting?"

He finishes eating quietly and then sits there. I know he's not going to leave until I talk.

The truth is, I was waiting for him.

But I still want him to mind his own business . . . after I ask him some questions.

"So, do you know how a fad works?"

He nods a little, shrugs a little. "I think so, at least the basics—something new shows up, everyone goes wild about it, everyone gets sick of it, and it's over. That seem right?"

"Sounds right. But how long does it take until everyone gets sick of something?"

"Depends. You've seen those fidget spinners?"

"Sure—there were tons at my school a while back, but hardly any now."

"Right, same at the high school. As a fad, it's over. It lasted pretty long because the companies making them kept coming up with changes. Like, the ones with LED lights? They were pretty slick. And another reason it lasted longer is because kids were plugged in to all the stuff about them online. Still, even though spinners were super popular, once a fad starts to die? *Click*—it disappears!"

"But let's say that you wanted a fad to die *before* everyone gets totally sick of it. Is there a way to end one?"

"Oh. So are we talking about buttons again?"

"Yes. Buttons again—more like *forever*."

"Hmm . . . Well, first of all, buttons aren't like Silly

Bandz or spinners—which kids have to go and buy. Almost anybody can get buttons, even if it's just a handful that they pull off some old clothes. Buttons are all over the place, mostly for free."

"Yeah, I know."

"And buttons aren't exactly a new invention either. So I guess a buttons fad is kind of a special case. But you're the one who's been seeing the whole thing play out at your school—what do *you* think is keeping it alive?"

"It's partly what you just said, that everybody's got some, and a lot of kids like trading them. There are so many different kinds, too. But . . . it's also that kids keep coming up with new things to do with them—making up games, and making crafty stuff, like bracelets. I heard that some fourth graders have been using wire to make button sculptures. And on the bus home today? I saw this boy, and he'd made a *snake* by stringing a couple hundred buttons onto a string—tiny buttons at the tail, then gradually larger ones toward the middle, then some different-sized ones to make the head. Kind of creepy, but also cool. And tomorrow button snakes could be all over the place . . . or little button frogs, or bugs—who knows? Because a spinner does *one* thing: It spins. Buttons can do anything that a kid can dream up. And everybody keeps wanting more and more buttons. And nobody seems to be getting sick of them either. Except me."

Ben sits perfectly still, staring at nothing.

Sometimes watching Ben feels like looking at myself

in a mirror, because right now? I know what he's doing: He just got an idea, and now he's working on a theory, or maybe a plan.

So I wait.

One thousand one, one thousand two, one thousand three, one thousand four . . .

And now Ben puts a serious look on his face.

"How much would you be willing to pay to kill the buttons fad?"

"*Pay?* What do you mean?"

"I mean, how badly do you want this fad to die? What would that be worth to you?"

"It'd be worth a lot."

"Okay, good. Next question: How much do you know about economics?"

"Uh, somewhere between almost nothing and nothing."

"Not a problem. But the first thing I want to say is this: I am not telling you to *do* anything, all right? I'm just going to explain a couple of concepts."

"About *economics?*"

"Yes, economics. It's very interesting, and I guarantee that after I explain some stuff, you're going to get an idea . . . about doing something. But I am not *telling* you to *do* anything."

"You've said that twice now."

"Because it's important."

I narrow my eyes until I'm almost squinting at him.

"It sounds like this *thing* that you are *not* telling me to do might be dangerous. Or get me into trouble. Or both. And *you* don't want to be held responsible."

Ben gives me a totally blank stare, no expression. "Do you want to learn something about economics or not?"

"Yes, O Great Teacher—teach me, *please* teach me!"

He ignores my sarcasm. "Okay. But remember—"

"I know: You're not telling me to *do* anything at all."

"Correct."

22

Supply and Demand

The windows along the north wall of the cafeteria face the grassy field behind the school, and from the table where I'm sitting with Hank, I've got a good view. It was raining this morning, but now it's sunny, so this is the first time on Wednesday that kids have been allowed outside to play.

"So, how come Grace's Gorgeous Goodies isn't open for business?" he asks.

"Um . . . what?"

"I *said,* you're not trading any buttons today—no sign. How come?"

"Oh, right. Taking a break."

Hank studies my face a moment and then turns around to stare out the windows, because that's what I'm doing.

And then he sees what I'm seeing.

About thirty fifth and sixth graders are half walking, half running around on the grass, then stopping to stoop down, and then repeating that process, over and over.

"What is going *on* out there?"

"Yeah, looks weird, doesn't it?"

I really can't say more than that, not without lying to Hank. Which I don't want to do.

Because the fact is, I know *exactly* what's going on out there.

Ben was right about economics—it's interesting. Especially the part about supply and demand, which was all he really wanted to explain.

He was like a college professor or something, completely serious, and yesterday after school our kitchen was his lecture hall.

"The concept of supply and demand is simple. If the supply of something is low, that means there's not much of it around, so it's scarce—and *that* makes it feel more valuable to people. And the idea that something is valuable? That's called *demand*—which is basically just the feeling that you want or need something."

I had no trouble understanding that, and Ben could tell, so he kept talking.

"Let's use doughnuts as an example. Imagine there was just one doughnut shop in our town, and that one shop made only *two* doughnuts each morning. That would be a very low supply, right? And because people really love delicious doughnuts, there would be a *lot* of people who wanted those two doughnuts—which means there would be very high demand. And instead of paying ninety-nine cents, a person might be willing to pay much more, maybe even five or ten dollars for *one* doughnut. Also, a lot of people might try to be the very first person at the door of the doughnut shop in the morning to buy a delicious doughnut—because there are only *two* in the whole town!"

I was still following along fine, but Ben wanted to be sure, so he flipped the situation around.

"*But* . . . what if there were fifteen doughnut shops in our town, and each shop made *one thousand* delicious doughnuts every morning? That would be a very high supply of doughnuts. So, would people feel like they had to rush to a doughnut shop to try to get one? No. And would people be willing to pay five dollars for one doughnut? No, because now there's a very high doughnut supply—fifteen thousand every morning! And if the supply gets really high like that, what happens to the demand—to that 'I've *got* to go get a doughnut right now!' feeling? It dies. There might even be so many doughnuts around that people would get sick of them. So, here's the most important idea: A very large supply of *anything* will kill the demand for that thing, no matter what it is."

Which was my favorite sentence of his whole economics lesson.

Then Ben stopped, and he looked me right in the eye, and he said that same sentence again, but much more slowly: "A very large supply of *anything* will *kill* the demand for that thing, no matter *what* it is."

As he'd been talking to me, Ben had also been doodling on a piece of notebook paper, drawing pictures of doughnuts and shop windows and trees and stuff. Which was a little distracting. But I was ready for the rest of his lecture.

"So that's the end of your economics lesson," Ben said with a smile.

"What? But . . . but you told me that I would get an idea, that I—"

He put up his hand. "Nope. I'm done. And I didn't tell you to do *anything*."

And then Ben slid his doodle paper across the table to me, grabbed his backpack, and walked out of the kitchen.

I was left sitting there, trying to remember everything he'd said and looking at the dumb little pictures he had drawn.

Ben's a terrible artist. A tree isn't that hard to draw, and neither is a shop window, but his pictures were so inaccurate. And I saw that he even messed up drawing something as simple as doughnuts, because two or three of his doughnuts were ridiculously small, and not only that, they had two holes instead of one.

Then I saw what my very smart big brother had done: Those weren't small doughnuts with two holes—he had drawn some buttons!

Just as Ben had promised, I got an idea. About doing something.

And it was sort of risky, and it was definitely scary.

But I did it anyway.

Last night, just after dark, I sneaked out of the house to our garage. I had carried four boxes of buttons down there from my room before dinner—three boxes of small gray buttons, plus one box of mixed bright colors. I loaded buttons into my camping backpack, strapped it on, and rode my bike seven blocks to school. Then I spread those buttons all around the playfield, throwing big handfuls again and again. I rode home, refilled my pack, and rode to school to fling buttons a second time, and then a third time, and a fourth time. The whole process took more than an hour—and I got back upstairs to my room just before Mom came to say good night.

So why did I scatter more than one hundred and fifty thousand buttons all over the playground? Because of economics: I did it to change the *supply* of buttons at Avery Elementary School!

By the time I finish my lunch, a crowd of fourth, fifth, and sixth graders are outside, grabbing up buttons—including Hank. It looks like one of those Easter egg hunts on the lawn at the White House. Even from this far away, I can see some bulging pockets stuffed with buttons.

According to my brother the economics professor, increasing the supply of buttons will kill the demand for buttons—that's the theory.

And I have successfully launched my real-life experiment.

So, now I have to wait and see what happens.

At the end of the day on Wednesday, it's a fact that now there are many, many more buttons at school, but they're mostly small and gray—except for about twenty thousand of the larger, brightly colored ones.

The final bell rings, and three fifth-grade girls come rushing up to me in the hall outside Mrs. Lang's room to trade their best Ellie's Originals for some of my special buttons.

By now Ellie has figured out what I've been doing, and she gives me a dirty look on her way past.

But these three trades are a surprise. I had expected that having so many more buttons around was going to shut off *all* the demand, like Ben said.

Then I see something: My *fancy* buttons are still scarce, so they're still in high demand. And it doesn't matter that they're surrounded by oceans of ordinary buttons. Also, demand for Ellie's Originals ought to stay high, because her stuff is all that I'm accepting in trade for my scarce, fancy buttons!

As I get on my bus, lots of the colorful new buttons from the playground are changing hands. And again, such active button trading surprises me.

I'm starting to think that my big economics experiment has resulted in only one real change: I now have four fewer boxes of buttons at home in my bedroom.

And, of course, I am still missing one best friend.

23

Into the Secret

I'm almost home on Wednesday afternoon, and my phone rings—the name *Hank* comes up on the screen. I don't really want to talk to him, but I also don't want to be rude.

"Hi, Hank."

"Hi. I just got home. I compared the buttons I picked up on the playground today to some of the buttons I got from your tray at lunch that first day we all brought stuff, and I'm pretty sure they're the same buttons."

I don't say anything, so he keeps talking.

"The colors, the material, the sizes, the design—they're all the same. And there's a tiny mold mark on the back of some of the dark red buttons—and the mark on the ones I got from you is identical to the mark on the ones I picked up outside on the field today."

"Interesting."

"Yes. Interesting. So, I think *you* spread those buttons

on the field at school. And I'd like to know if that's true. I'd also like to know if this is part of your war against Ellie."

"Um . . . I'd rather not say."

"Oh. Okay, fine. Have a nice day."

"Wait! Don't hang up."

"I'm still here."

"You're right—I did put the buttons around on the playground, but it's not part of my war with Ellie. It's an experiment to see if I can stop the fad. I'm just . . . I want it to stop."

"And you think flooding the school with *more* buttons is supposed to make them disappear? Doesn't make sense."

"Well, Ben told me some stuff about supply and demand, and if the supply of something goes way up, then the demand is supposed to go way down. For example, if there were thousands of doughnuts everywhere, people would get sick of them and wouldn't want them as much."

"Yeah . . . I see how that might work with doughnuts. But what if this fad is more like a forest fire—and *you* just added a lot more trees?"

"Like I said, it's an experiment."

"Right. I get that. But . . . how many buttons did you put out on the field?"

I almost say, *I'd rather not talk about it.*

But I don't.

"Can you come over here?"

"To your house? Now?"

"Yes, now. To my house."

When the doorbell rings, Mom and I get there at the same time.

"Hi, Mrs. Hamlin. Hi, Grace."

Hank's out of breath from his bike ride, but I'm glad it took him a while to get here. My clothes are all put away for the first time in weeks.

"Come on in, Hank. It's nice to see you."

He nods at my mom. "Thanks—good to see you, too."

She's a little surprised. I didn't tell her he was coming.

"Hank came over to see my . . . collection. In my room. And if we want any snacks, we'll get them ourselves, okay?"

"Sure, that's fine. I'll just be in my office."

My room looks less messy now, but my closet is still a wreck, so I moved the three boxes of buttons out of there and stacked them in front of my tall bookcase.

Hank stands still, just inside my door, and slowly looks around.

It's been a long time since I've had a new friend in my room. But no one else really paid much attention to my stuff. Hank looks like he's scanning every single object, sort of the way my new phone takes a panoramic photo.

He points at my dresser. "I'd recognize *those* anywhere!"

He walks over and picks up the blue glass jar full of small gray buttons.

"I've got at least this many at *my* house—the exact same buttons!"

"Yeah, I dumped a *lot* of them on the playground."

"So . . . you got them from the mill, right? In Massachusetts?"

"Good guess."

"More like a deduction. You showed some buttons along with the other stuff you got from the mill, so I figured you must have gotten more than you brought to school. And from the start, you've always had plenty—plus you never seemed worried about giving buttons away."

He nods at the stack in front of the bookcase. "Are there more in those boxes?"

"Yes. More buttons."

"So, how many buttons did you dump at school?"

"Four boxes."

"Wow! And you've still got *three* huge boxes left?"

"Actually, you should look under my bed."

"No—*really*?"

"Really."

Hank drops to the floor, lifts the dust ruffle, then lets out a long, low whistle. "*Whoa!* Is it okay if I pull some of these out and see what you've got here?"

"Sure—you can look at all of them."

I sit back in my big encyclopedia armchair as Hank opens box after box. And now I know how my mom and dad feel when they watch me opening presents.

On his fourth box, Hank finds some fancy buttons.

"Look at *these*—I can't believe it!"

"Yeah, I love those—and I've got two other boxes like that."

"No *way*! Some of these are worth a *fortune*! These bright red-and-yellow Bakelites? *One* of these would sell for ten dollars—and you've got a dozen, *and* they're still on the original store display card!"

Five or six boxes later, Ben shows up in my doorway.

"Hank—long time no see! So . . . did Grace make you take the oath of silence? About not telling anyone that she's a crackpot button hoarder?"

Hank looks lost. He shakes his head.

"Very funny, Ben. You can go now."

"Because she made *me* swear that I wouldn't tell a soul. You must be a *very* special young man."

"Mom! Ben's bothering us!"

She calls up the stairs, "Ben—come here, please."

"Coming, Mother." Ben grins at us. "Well, you two have fun, all right?"

I'm blushing nine shades of pink, but Hank doesn't seem to notice. He's already deep into a fresh box of brilliant-blue celluloid buttons, comparing all the different sizes.

After the last box is opened, Hank leans back against the end of my bed, his long legs stretched out straight on the floor.

"*Whew*—your grandfather sent all these from Massachusetts?"

"Yup—they arrived the first week of school. On a big wooden pallet."

He's quiet for a moment, then says, "I know Ben was teasing, but does anyone else know you've got all these?"

"Me, Grampa, my mom and dad, Ben, and now you. That's it."

"Well, you're *not* a crackpot! If Ben had any idea how much money these are worth, he wouldn't be making fun of you!"

"Yeah, but until you told me, I didn't know they were worth anything. I just wanted them, just . . . to *have*. So I might be a little goofy after all."

"But the buttons fit right in—with all your other stuff, I mean. Everything you have, it's all . . . really interesting."

He gets to his feet.

"I should put all these boxes away now. I told my mom I'd be home by four."

"That's all right—I'll shove them under the bed later. And while everything's out, go ahead and take whatever you want. For your collection."

"Oh, I couldn't do that. But thanks for the offer."

"I'm serious—take some. There's a plastic bag right there on my dresser."

He goes to the dresser and finds the bag. And then he stops and picks up something else.

"This is that pinwheel button! What happened?"

I shrug. "It broke."

He's got the three pieces up close, studying them.

"This didn't just break. . . . I can see marks on it, like it got jammed into a crack and then bent sideways, or maybe hit with something. This is tough material, so it took a lot of force to snap the pieces like this."

He looks at me, questions in his eyes.

I don't want to explain. But I don't want to lie to him. At all.

So I take a deep breath and tell him everything—me giving the button back to Brooke, her trading it for a new bracelet, and then me getting the button from Ellie again, broken. And then me getting the new bracelet from Brooke—for revenge.

"And there on the dresser, that folded paper? That's the little handmade envelope Ellie used to return it."

He picks it up, reads the note, puts it back.

"And now you and Ellie are at war."

"Yeah."

"And you're also sick of buttons."

"Yes."

"This explains a lot. Thanks for telling me."

"Except I don't *want* to be at war with Ellie!"

He smiles at me. "Yeah, I knew that."

"You *did*?"

"Yeah."

I can't think what to say next.

He puts the plastic bag back on my dresser. "Listen, I'll get some of these buttons later, okay? I've really got to leave now."

"Okay."

I follow him down the staircase and outside onto the front porch.

"Thanks again," he says. "For asking me to come over."

"You're welcome."

"I'll see you tomorrow."

"Yup—see you tomorrow."

I watch him pedal away—a little tall, a little awkward, his helmet perched on his head.

And as much as I don't want to be at war with Ellie anymore, if all these problems and all this stupid drama are the price I needed to pay to get to know Hank better? Then I don't have any regrets.

Not one.

24

Courage

I'm setting the kitchen table before dinner when Dad comes in with a box under his arm.

"The UPS driver just left this out front—it's addressed to you and your mother."

He hands me a package about the size of a shoebox.

"It's from Grampa!"

Ben says, "Here's a wild guess: more buttons."

And I know Ben's right.

Mom moves the salad bowl off the counter. "Put it here!"

She's more excited than I am, and the knife she uses to slit the tape still has juice on it from cutting tomatoes.

"Oh yeah . . . just like I said—more *buttons*!" Ben is so pleased with himself. I have to resist telling him he's sort of been acting like a jerk today.

But I can't resist a different comment.

"Yes, you're a *genius* at predicting the contents of

packages—a lot better than you are at predicting the effects of adjusting supply and demand . . . like with that thing that you *told* me to do."

"I . . . I never told you to do *anything*!"

"What did Ben tell you to do?"

Dad seems very interested.

"Oh, nothing. I'm just teasing—right, Ben?"

"Yeah, you're hilarious!"

Inside the box are two envelopes laid on top of the buttons, one addressed to each of us. Mom opens hers and begins reading aloud, and I can see Grampa's handwriting on the cream-colored notepaper.

Dear Carolyn,

After some gentle prompting from Grace, I've begun sorting through your mother's upstairs sitting room and study. These buttons were with her sewing things. They reach back several generations, and you'll probably be able to spot a few from some of your old clothes. If you have any questions about any of the other buttons, I'm sure Grace can teach you all you need to know!

Over the next few months, I'll be sending along a few things that you might want to keep. All the rest will be going to a local charity, where I hope they'll do some good.

This process was hard for me to begin, but now that I'm well into it, I'm finding so many happy memories, especially of the years when you and your brothers shared this home with us.

Thanks for being such a wonderful daughter, and I
hope we can all get together this fall or winter.
                    With all my love,
                    Dad

Mom's voice is shaky as she finishes, and she has to brush away a tear. But she makes herself smile.

"Such a sweet, sweet man. So, let's hear your letter, Grace."

But I don't want to get emotional in front of everyone, and I probably would.

"Um . . . I'd rather open it later. Is that okay?"

"Sure, that's fine."

After dinner and the kitchen cleanup, I've got Gramma's buttons upstairs, laid out across my bedspread.

Grampa was right—they go back to the 1800s. I spot five or six bone buttons right away, plus dozens of shoe buttons, a category we had to add when Hank and I were sorting our thrift store collection. A shoe button looks sort of like a small pea that's been sliced in half, with a rounded top and a flat back. Shoe buttons are usually black, with one little wire loop on the back side. Interesting, but I've seen plenty of buttons recently. What I really need right now is words.

And as I begin reading the letter, I can hear Grampa's voice, strong and clear and kind.

Dear Grace,

Well, I finally found the courage to go through your grandmother's things. Courage might sound like a strange word to choose, but being here in the world on my own again is a new experience, and sometimes it can feel a little scary. However, I'm finding that new experiences seem to be exactly what I need.

Speaking of newness, our mill building is looking less and less like a graveyard every day! The outside brick has been sandblasted clean, a crew of masons is making sure the walls are sound and weatherproof, and some of the new windows have already been installed. I'll text pictures soon!

I hope that sometime you'll tell me a little more about your friend Hank. How's that going? I also hope that you and the unforgettable Miss Emerson have gotten back onto common ground. From my brief time meeting her, I can guess she's not always an easy person to be with. But sometimes friends who make demands on us are the ones worth keeping—and sometimes they're also the ones who most need a true friend. You'll know what's best.

As I'm sure you can understand, a grandmother is not allowed to pick favorite grandchildren. But I know for certain that you have a very special place in your grandmother Marjorie's heart, just as you do in mine. And that will never change.

Our time together was the best week of my summer,

*and I can't wait till you come back for the <u>Grand
Reopening of Burnham Mills</u>—keep your suitcase handy!*

> *With all my love,*
> *Grampa*

I cried at the funeral last summer, but this feels different. I'm crying now because I love Grampa, and I'm crying because Gramma would be disappointed in me, and I'm crying because both of them would tell me I've been mean to Ellie. And I have. Trying to end the fad? Totally selfish. Everyone else is having fun, and Ellie's being creative, and kids are making things and learning all kinds of stuff, and what am I doing? I'm acting mean and stupid and selfish and spoiled—everything I've accused Ellie of being. And I'm also crying because Hank was so sweet this afternoon. He knew that I don't want to be at war with Ellie anymore—he *knew* that.

The tears have made some little splashes on Grampa's letter, and I finally stop. But I don't stop thinking. Because unless I *do* something, the tears will be a lie—like making a promise and not keeping it.

So I put Gramma's buttons back into their box.

Then I do my homework, still thinking.

I hug my mom when she comes to say good night—a long hug.

And I keep thinking and thinking.

And by the time I begin to fall asleep, I know what I need to do.

25

Melting

Ellie's face looks like she might shove me off the sidewalk. Or worse.

So I say it again, as sincerely as I can: "We really need to talk—please?"

"*Fine.*"

She's cold and suspicious, but I was expecting that. I also knew we wouldn't be able to talk out here with all the buses arriving.

"Let's go inside to the library, okay?"

"Whatever."

I picked the library because we'll have to be quiet in there—less chance that we might start yelling at each other.

I hold the door open, and Ellie walks in and then turns right.

So far, so good.

But I can see the stiffness in each step, impatience in every gesture. Ellie's looking for a fight.

And even though I tried to prepare for this logically, I know that this isn't like solving a math problem.

It's more like untangling a knot. Or maybe melting an iceberg.

Inside the library, I walk to a table way in the back, and Ellie follows and sits down across from me.

"What do you want?"

It's a sharp challenge, but I don't react. I keep to my plan.

"First I want to say something . . . about this." And I open my hand to show her the pieces of the broken pinwheel button. "When I pushed my way into the middle of your trade with Brooke, that was totally wrong. And selfish. And I'm sorry I did it, and I hope someday you'll forgive me."

Ellie starts to say something, but I quickly pull a brown envelope out of my backpack and empty it onto the table between us.

"Eighteen bracelets, three necklaces, and two anklets. All made by you."

She tries to hide it, but she's surprised.

"I . . . I knew you had some of these, but I didn't know it was so many. Why were you . . ."

"Because I was mad at you for breaking the pinwheel button, and for not letting me sit with you at lunch."

"I still don't see . . ."

"I was going to smash all the buttons with a hammer, and cut all the ribbons to bits, and then give the pieces back to you. To get even."

"*Really? You* were going to do that?"

"Yes, until I saw that this whole mess was actually my own dumb fault."

"Well . . . I *did* break the pinwheel, and then I sent it back with that note. Which was super mean of me."

"Yeah, but yesterday, when I thought about how mad *you* had to be to break the button that way, and that *I* had gotten you that upset? I felt so bad for you that it made me cry. I'm really sorry I made you so angry."

Ellie shakes her head. "But *I'm* the one who makes everybody mad . . . because I show off too much. Don't you think that's true, that I show off too much?"

It's a dangerous question. But I have to be honest.

"Well . . . maybe . . . sometimes. But you *do* have a lot of very cool stuff. And if *I* had as many beautiful things as you do? I might have trouble not showing off, too."

"You?" Ellie gives me a smile, the kind that melts icebergs. "No way, that's just not *like* you—it's not. And that's how *I* want to be!"

I feel a lump in my throat, but I don't want to start blubbering. So it's good that the first bell rings.

We pick up our things and head for the hallway, and it feels like the struggles of the past week never happened. But, of course, they did. And because they did, I don't think Ellie and I have ever been better friends than we are right now. Walking together toward homeroom feels like the most natural thing in the world.

"So, at lunch today, do you maybe want to come over and sit with me and Hank?"

Ellie smiles again, playful this time.

"I've *noticed* you and Hank!"

I don't answer, but just kind of lean her way so that our shoulders bump. And then we both burst out laughing.

Right before we get to the room, she says, "So, what are you going to do with all my bracelets and stuff?"

"I'm going to try to remember who I got them from and give them back. For free."

"See? That's what I mean about you. I think *I* would have used them for trading all over again!"

"Oh, I thought about that, believe me. Kids really love these things. But I've got enough buttons to last a lifetime—I'm kind of tired of them."

"Yeah, I get that. But . . . do you have any like *this* yet?"

And she pulls a brilliant red-and-white button out of her pocket and hands it to me. It's vintage celluloid, and the two colors are swirled to look like an old-fashioned peppermint lollipop.

Then Ellie says, "Oops! See? I'm showing off again—I can't help it!"

"Actually . . . this button? It started out as mine, and I've got tons more like it, some even prettier. This is the kind of button I've been trading with."

"What do you mean?"

"I mean, the way I got kids to give me all your bracelets and necklaces was by trading with buttons like *this*!"

Ellie pulls six other buttons from her pockets. "And these?"

I look and then nod. "All except that big green one started out belonging to me!"

"So that means *I've* been trading *my* bracelets to get more of *your* buttons, and *you've* been trading *your* buttons to get more of *my* bracelets!"

We both start laughing again, and then I say, "But *I* was going to crush your bracelets to bits!" And somehow that seems hilarious now.

We sort of stumble into homeroom together, and we'd have kept on laughing, but the PA speaker up on the wall makes a loud *ding,* and everyone gets quiet.

"Good morning. This is Mrs. Porter, and I have an important announcement about a change in our schedule for today. At eight-forty-five, everyone in grades one through six is to come to the auditorium for an assembly. Sixth-grade students should stay with their homeroom teachers rather than go to first-period classes. Thank you, and I will see you soon."

Ellie looks at me. "I wonder what *that's* about."

"Yeah, me too."

I say that, but I would bet a hundred dollars that I know *exactly* what the principal wants to talk about today.

26

Consequences

At every big assembly, the lower grades sit down near the stage, and the upper grades stack up toward the back of the auditorium. So this is the first year I've ever sat in the very back row. And I have to say, I like it back here. I feel sort of hidden.

Mrs. Porter is on the stage, and the room gets quiet as she steps to the microphone.

"Good morning, girls and boys, and thank you for finding your seats in such a calm and orderly way. I've asked you here to talk about buttons."

There's a quick buzz of chatter and a little bit of laughing, but Mrs. Porter shakes her head and frowns, and the auditorium goes silent again.

"Over the past week or so, many of you have become very interested in buttons. But with almost every fad that finds its way to school, there comes a moment when that fad begins to get in the way of our work. And we have now reached that moment. Therefore, starting tomorrow morning, any buttons that are seen here at school will be taken away by your teachers and will be held for you until the end of the school year. And today I expect any of you who may have buttons here at school to take them home and *leave* them at home. Of course, I'm not talking about the buttons we all wear each day, but the buttons that are being traded and collected and used as toys and game pieces. So I'm going to say this again: I expect all of you who have buttons here at school today to take those buttons home with you this afternoon and leave them there. Please raise your hand now if you understand what I have just asked everyone to do."

I put my hand up in the air, and so does every other kid in the auditorium.

So . . . that's it. My wish has come true. Mrs. Porter says that the buttons fad is over, so it is—at least at school.

"You may put your hands down now, and thank you all very much."

The auditorium is filled with a sudden buzz, because every kid here knows that the assembly is over. Some of the younger kids down front even begin to stand up.

"Please, quiet—quiet, and take your seats."

The room gets quiet, but it's not the same full silence as before. And it makes me wonder if anyone has ever done a scientific study about large groups of children all together in the same room. Because this makes me remember a nature show about bees that Grampa and I watched, and how any little disturbance will go rippling right through a whole beehive.

Mrs. Porter has more to say, but now the bees are restless.

"As many of you know, a very large quantity of buttons was found on our school playground on Wednesday."

That one sentence sets off a burst of chatter, a lot of nodding, a lot of reaching into pockets.

That one sentence also makes my stomach tighten up into a knot.

Ellie's sitting right next to me, and I'm afraid she's going to be able to hear my heart as it thumps inside my chest, my throat, my head.

"Quiet, please, everyone settle down. I know that a lot of you picked up buttons when you were outside yesterday, but there were still many left on the ground. After school, I walked around with our custodian and with the town employees who mow the grass. They were concerned that the buttons might damage the lawn mowers. And when they began mowing, several cars stopped to complain that bits of buttons had struck their cars as they drove past. I had to call the police and ask them to close off the street next to the playground until the mowing was finished."

I'm trying to sit very still, trying not to breathe too fast, trying not to faint, trying not to jump out of my seat and run screaming from the auditorium.

And Mrs. Porter keeps talking.

"After the mowing was finished, two police officers and I studied the school's security video recordings from Tuesday night. We saw that someone came into the schoolyard, not once or twice, but *four* times to throw buttons all over the field. It was dark when this happened, so it was impossible to identify the person who did this. The police department is now calling this a case of littering on public property, and they have opened an investigation. Any student who has information that might help the police should speak to a teacher or to me."

A deep hush settles over the auditorium.

Mrs. Porter lets the silence go on.

And on.

My jaw is clamped so tightly I feel like I might crush my teeth.

Hank is sitting in the row ahead of me, about three seats to the left. I'm just praying that he doesn't turn around and wink, or smile, or give me a thumbs-up. But he's too smart to do something like that.

Actually . . . *he's* probably freaked out, too! If you know about a crime, then *you're* just as guilty as the person who did it!

Unless you tell.

Finally, Mrs. Porter speaks.

"I want to thank you all for paying such careful attention this morning. The first graders may leave now, and everyone else, please remain seated until your teachers ask you to stand up."

The auditorium begins to buzz again, and Ellie whispers, "*Somebody's* going to need a lawyer! Or not. The fine for littering can't be a big deal, right? Maybe like a hundred dollars or something? Anyway, pretty exciting, don't you think?"

My mouth is so dry I can barely talk.

"Yeah . . . it's exciting."

But the correct word is *terrifying*—it's terrifying!

I've *never* been in trouble at school before, never been sent to the principal, never had to stay after school—I can't even remember the last time a teacher yelled at me! And *this*? This is *real* trouble . . . the kind where parents have to come for a meeting in the principal's office!

And the police will be there—the *police*!

As this thought slams into my skull, Hank turns around and catches my eye.

I smile and try to look brave and calm.

And totally fail.

I don't know if Hank looks worried or sad. Or terrified.

Like me.

But I know one thing for sure—I can't sit still for one more second.

I whisper to Ellie, "See you in social studies," and then I stand up and scooch my way along the row of kids until I get to Mrs. Lang, who's standing in the aisle.

"Mrs. Lang, may I go to the office? I . . . I don't feel well."

Which is not a lie. I've never felt worse in my life.

She stares into my face for a second, and I can see the flash of concern in her eyes. I must look awful.

"Of course—you go right ahead, Grace. Do you need someone to walk with you?"

"No, I'll be okay. Thanks."

The halls are filled with third and fourth graders leaving the auditorium, but I barely see them, can barely feel my feet on the tile floor.

And when I get to the office, the doors leading outside are just to the right, and I feel like making a break for it, like a convict in a prison movie.

But I don't.

In the main office, the school secretary looks away from her computer screen and gives me a big smile. "Hi, Grace. What can I help you with?"

In second grade, and again in fourth, I got picked a lot whenever my teachers needed to send something to the office. Because I was such a good little girl. Back then.

So I know Mrs. Sterling pretty well.

"I have to talk with Mrs. Porter, please."

"She just got back from the assembly, and there's a busy morning ahead. Can this wait until lunchtime, say about twelve-fifteen?"

"I really have to talk to her now. It's about the buttons. On the field."

Mrs. Sterling's eyebrows jump halfway up her forehead. "Oh. I see. Just sit over there on the bench, and I'll tell Mrs. Porter you're here."

I've looked into the office and seen kids sitting on this bench before, and I always felt sorry for them. And now I'm feeling sorry for me.

Mrs. Porter's door opens, and she gives me a smile.

"Good morning, Grace. Please come in and have a seat there at the table."

It's a small round table to the left of her desk, and I take the chair facing the window that looks out at the bus turnaround.

Mrs. Porter sits across from me. She's not a scary person. She reminds me of Mom's friend Carla—warm, friendly, nice smile.

Mrs. Porter is wearing a gray wool skirt and jacket with a pale blue shirt.

And right away, I start counting the buttons—I can't help myself.

"So. You wanted to see me, right?"

Before I can answer, there's a knock at the door, and Mrs. Sterling opens it and sticks her head inside. "Sorry to interrupt."

She walks over and bends down and whispers something into the principal's ear.

And this time, it's Mrs. Porter's eyebrows that go shooting upward.

She looks at me and says, "It seems that we need more chairs at our table."

I'm confused, and Mrs. Porter is on her feet, getting chairs.

I look over at the doorway, and suddenly I'm *really* confused.

Because two kids walk into the office and sit down— Hank Powell on my right and Ellie Emerson on my left.

27

Deal

All my logic, all my ability to reason and think like a scientist, none of that is working. But I feel like I have to say something anyway, so I say it fast.

"Mrs. Porter, I don't know what Ellie and Hank are doing here, because they didn't have anything to do with those buttons outside on the playground. I put them there by myself, and it was totally my idea. So they shouldn't even be here. At all."

She looks from Hank to Ellie. "Is that true—that Grace put those buttons on the playground completely by herself?"

They both nod, and Mrs. Porter says, "Then it seems like this matter is between Grace and me—and her parents. So, why are you here? Hank, you first."

"We're here because we're witnesses. Grace wasn't littering. She was just giving away a lot of buttons. And the only reason she was doing that was to try to stop the fad, which is the same thing *you* wanted—right?"

"And how do you happen to know all this?"

"Because yesterday I went over to Grace's house after school, and she told me that she was the one who put the buttons on the field, and she explained why she did it. It was an experiment about supply and demand. Because if the supply of something goes up, then the demand for it is supposed to go down. And she wanted the demand for buttons to go all the way down to zero. So the fad would be over. And when I saw Grace heading for the office a few minutes ago, I told Ellie everything, and here we are."

Mrs. Porter looks at me. "Why did you want the fad to end?"

Ellie raises her hand and starts talking before I can say a word.

"So, I've been best friends with Grace ever since second grade, but last week? We got into an argument about this pretty button that we both wanted, and Grace traded for it before I could, so then I was really mean to her, and she was really mean back to me, and it just kept getting worse and worse and worse, and we were both miserable about everything, but *then* Grace decided to actually *do* something to make the whole buttons thing go away, so that we could be friends again. And that's why it wasn't littering."

Mrs. Porter starts to say something, but Hank jumps in again.

"And Ellie and Grace and I? We'll go over the whole

playground every day after school, and we'll keep on working until every single button out there is picked up."

Mrs. Porter shakes her head. "Actually, that won't be necessary. After mowing yesterday, the crew went back over the area with a leaf vacuum, and there are hardly any buttons left."

Ellie says, "Then Hank and Grace and I will chip in and we'll pay for the extra time it took them to vacuum up the buttons, and we'll also pay what it cost to have the police close off the street during the mowing—how about that? Is it a deal? Can we shake on it?"

Ellie leans forward and puts her hand out toward Mrs. Porter.

Then Hank puts out his hand, and so do I.

And Mrs. Porter? She's surprised.

But she smiles, and she shakes with each of us—Ellie, Hank, and then me.

Except after we shake, she keeps hold of my hand.

"I'll call the police department, and after I explain, I'll ask them to drop their investigation. That ought to be the end of it."

I can't keep my eyes from filling up. "Thanks, Mrs. Porter."

She nods at Ellie and Hank. "They're the ones you should thank. It's a great thing to have *one* good friend, but to have *two* looking out for you? That's nothing short of wonderful. Now, go ask Mrs. Sterling for passes, and get back to class. And have a happy day."

We're out of the office in less than a minute, walking together toward the sixth-grade hall.

And with Ellie on my left and Hank on my right, I have to agree with Mrs. Porter: This is nothing short of wonderful.

28

One More Button

Mrs. Porter's total button ban happened at that all-school assembly almost a month ago, but this morning on the bus? I saw button trading. Not as much as back in September, and not out in the open, but it's still happening. Turns out that a fad is a tough thing to kill.

So is a friendship. Which is not a theory—I have proof.

Because it's Friday afternoon one week before Halloween, and in about five minutes Ellie and I are meeting up for the only sleepover we've had since last May.

And it's at *my* house—which hasn't happened for *years*!

Walking back to class after Hank and Ellie came and rescued me in the principal's office, I felt happier than I could ever remember.

And over the next few days, Ellie and I talked, really *talked*, maybe for the first time ever. I told her about

Grampa's mill building, and about the buttons he sent me, and about Gramma and graveyards and what my mom said about dying and not dying, and how she said that she wasn't friends today with a single kid she knew when she was in sixth grade—we talked about everything.

I could tell Hank kind of felt left out when Ellie and I got going, especially at lunchtime. So Hank and I have been texting. A lot. And in our science and math classes every day? Ellie's not there, which is good.

The day Mrs. Porter called us to the office and handed us the bill for the button cleanup expenses? That was a tough one.

We got into the hallway afterward, and Ellie exploded.

"*Six hundred dollars?* That's two hundred dollars *each*—I don't have that kind of money! I mean, I've got all my birthday cash, but it's in a savings account, and if I tried to take out that much, my parents would have a fit! *Six hundred dollars?* That has to be wrong!"

Of course, Mrs. Porter wasn't wrong at all. Four people doing lawn work for three hours at $22.50 per hour, plus three police officers on special detail for two hours at $55.00 per hour equals $600.00. That's the math, and numbers don't lie.

But Hank wasn't worried, and neither was I. The two of us had already worked out a solution. And once we told Ellie about our plan, she stopped worrying, too.

Okay, it was really Hank's plan.

Because Hank was the one who had been doing tons of

research about buttons, and he knew that vintage buttons are valuable, and he knew that there are active collectors on eBay, hunting for buttons and buying them every single day. And he knew that I had *plenty* of valuable buttons.

Except we had a problem: A person has to be at least eighteen years old to have an eBay account. Ben is only fifteen, so he was useless. And there was no way that we wanted to get any of our parents involved.

"You want me to do *what*?"

That's what Grampa said when the three of us ambushed him on speakerphone one afternoon and explained how we needed him to open up an eBay account and a PayPal account for us so we could earn six hundred dollars by selling vintage buttons.

Grampa said no about twenty times, but one great thing about Ellie? She can talk faster than anybody, and she never gives up. And once Grampa started laughing, that was it, and our top secret after-school button-selling business was off and running.

I gave Hank bags and bags of buttons so he could do research and organize sets of buttons to offer for sale. Next, I took lots of photos of each button group to show what we were selling, and then I emailed the pics to Ellie so she could write descriptions and do the computer work to put each group up for sale in our eBay store.

And Grampa? He just kept working on his old mill building—and worrying about how he was going to explain all this to Mom and Dad if they found out what he'd done.

And they did find out.

Because once the buttons started to sell, orders piled up fast, and then we had to mail little packages of buttons all over the place—and I mean *all* over. Like to England and Japan and the Netherlands, even to China. And there was no way to keep all that a secret.

So I had to explain to Mom and Dad *what* we were doing, and then *why* we were doing it, and then *how* we were doing it. And Grampa was part of the how.

They were pretty upset about the why, because I told them everything—only I didn't tell about Ben's economics lecture and the way he *didn't* tell me to do anything.

Ben owes me big-time. And he knows it.

But Mom and Dad understood why I dumped all those buttons, and they were glad everything was good again between Ellie and me. And when I told them how I had *two* best friends come and stand up for me in the principal's office, Dad's opinion of Hank went from high to higher—which Hank totally deserves.

The balance in our PayPal account reached $607.14 after only eleven days of button trading, and the stuff we sold barely made a dent in my three boxes of specialty buttons.

After we had paid Mrs. Porter, Ellie wanted to keep on selling. Her idea was that I would keep 50 percent of the profits because the buttons were mine, and she and Hank would each get 25 percent for the work they did. It seemed fair, but I told her that I was all done with buttons, at least for now.

So Ellie didn't get her way, but she didn't get mad, and she didn't keep pushing, and she didn't stomp away in a huff—which was something really new.

And really good.

I've got the front door open before Ellie can ring the bell, and we both wave goodbye to her mom.

Inside the front hall, she looks around.

"It feels like it's been *forever* since I was here!"

"Not forever—just two years, one month, and six days. You came over after school to work on a project for social studies."

She nods. "Right—fourth grade, and it was about the Illinois Constitution!" Then she looks at me. "And ever since then, I always made you come to *my* house. You know how come I did that?"

"Of course—so you could be in charge of *everything*."

We both laugh a little, but she gets serious again because she knows I'm actually not joking about that.

"So how come you kept putting up with me?"

"Simple—I've always known that you're a really good person. Plus I love that fancy root beer your mom buys!"

We laugh again and then go upstairs.

Ellie stops in the doorway of my room, just looking around. Which is exactly what Hank did that day he came over.

I had started to clean things up when I got home after

school today, but then I stopped. Because I wanted my room to look the way it is, not the way I imagined Ellie would like it to look.

She walks over to my dresser, and I stand a little to one side, watching her eyes jump around from object to object. I hope she's not trying to make sense of it all, because that's not possible, even for me.

Then Ellie points, and I see what she's found: The three jagged pieces of the pinwheel button. Just like Hank did.

"Sorry. I meant to throw those away."

"No, you shouldn't. Listen, I know you're pretty tired of buttons, but I brought you one more anyway."

She hands me a brass button. I run my thumb across the raised letters on the front—STRONG HOLD. And right away, I remember.

"I can't keep this—it came from your great-great-grandfather!"

She smiles at me. "You know what your mom said, about losing touch with all her sixth-grade friends? Well, we're *not* going to be like that. If I ever need this button, you'll be the first to know. And if that day comes, then you have to show up *in person* and give it back to me."

Ellie puts out her hand.

"Deal?"

"Deal!"

And we shake on it.

Author's Note

Dear Reader,

As a kid, I used to poke around in tumbledown barns and sheds, especially in rural Maine, and if I happened to spot a rusty ax-head or a broken doorknob or some strange chunk of brass or iron or glass, it was like a treasure to me, and it would follow me home. As those who know me today will tell you, I still can't resist old tools and odd bits of this and that. My office is loaded with all kinds of interesting and semi-useless stuff that I've found or bought over the decades.

Many years ago I worked in an old textiles mill that was soon to be remodeled into apartments, and my company was the last one still in the building. One day as I looked through some junk left in a hallway, I found a box of buttons—blue, gray, and brown, all about the size of a quarter. There were probably two or three hundred buttons of each color. So I took them home and gave them to our young sons. Instantly all four of them went bonkers about buttons.

The boys divided them up (mostly by grabbing, as I recall), and then those buttons were used as money during card games, for creating strange sculptures with wire and thread, for bartering and trading, and, of course, for throwing at each other. The blue buttons mysteriously became more valuable than the brown ones, and the brown ones were more prized than the gray. There was a lot of arguing, a lot of hoarding and hiding, and there were many loud accusations of unfairness and greediness and outright robbery. And then, after only six or seven days, everyone moved on, and those beloved buttons were nothing more than a nuisance littering the floor of the basement playroom.

During the seven years I was a classroom teacher, I saw a number of fads come and go—Mexican jumping beans, Pet Rocks, mood rings, Wizzzer tops, and Star Wars action figures, to name a few. And during the years our sons grew up, my wife and I saw many more fads arrive and exit, from Pokémon cards to Beanie Babies to Silly Bandz. But when I got the idea to write a story about a fad at a middle school, the first memory that skidded into my head was the way our own kids had reacted to that box of buttons. And the result of this happy mental collision is the book you have in your hands: *The Friendship War*.

Thanks for taking this little journey with me and for helping to make reading the one fad that will never die!

Acknowledgments

I want to thank Steve Smith of Cornish, Maine, for helping me find most of the buttons that provided background and inspiration for parts of this book. I also want to thank my editor, Shana Corey, for being a cheerful fount of good ideas; my agent, Amy Berkower, for her steadfast help and invaluable advice; and all the talented and dedicated people at Random House Children's Books for their enthusiastic work on my behalf. I am especially thankful for my wife, Rebecca, whose love and unfailing support make every day far happier and much more productive than it would otherwise be.

If you liked The Friendship War, *don't miss*

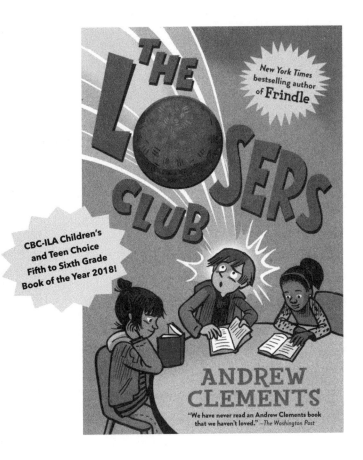

Words like *loser* and *bookworm*—they're just labels, right?
And labels don't tell the whole story.
Can the Losers Club members take their story back?
Turn the page for an excerpt!

CHAPTER 1

What Happens Next?

A bright red plastic chair sat in the hallway outside the door of the principal's office. This chair was known as the Hot Seat, and at nine-fifteen on a Tuesday morning, Alec Spencer was in it.

During his years at Bald Ridge Elementary School, Alec had visited the Hot Seat a lot—he had lost count somewhere in the middle of fifth grade. This morning's visit was the very first time he'd been sent to the principal's office during sixth grade . . . except this was also the very first day of school, so Alec had been a sixth grader for less than forty-five minutes.

A kid could end up in the Hot Seat at least a hundred different ways, most of them pretty standard: talking back to a teacher, bullying or shoving or punching, throwing food in the cafeteria—stuff like that.

But Alec was a special case. Every time he had landed in the Hot Seat, he had been caught doing something that teachers usually liked: reading. It wasn't about *what* he was reading or *how* he was reading—it was always because of *where* and *when* he was reading.

Maybe his mom and dad were to blame for spending all those hours reading to him when he was little. Or maybe *The Sailor Dog* was to blame, or *The Very Hungry Caterpillar,* or possibly *The Cat in the Hat.* But there was no doubt that Alec had loved books from the get-go. Once he found a beginning, he had to get to the middle, because the middle always led to the end of the story. And no matter what, Alec had to know what happened next.

Today's situation was a perfect example. Just twenty minutes earlier, Alec had been in first-period art class, and Ms. Boden had passed out paper and pencils to everyone. Then she said, "I want each of you to make a quick sketch of this bowl of apples, and don't put your name on your paper. In five minutes I'm going to collect the sketches and tape them up on the wall, and then we're going to talk about what we see. All right? Please begin."

From across the art room, Alec had looked like he was hunched over his paper, hard at work. But when Ms. Boden got closer, she had discovered that Alec was hunched over a book, reading—something that had happened many, many times in past years. So Ms. Boden instantly sent him off to see the principal.

The second-period bell rang, and the hallway outside the principal's office filled up with kids—which was one of the worst parts of being in the Hot Seat. If you got sent to see Mrs. Vance, the whole school knew about it.

However, Alec wasn't just sitting there on the Hot Seat. He was also reading. It was a book called *The High King*, and in his mind, Alec held a sword in his hand as he ran along beside the main character, battling to save a kingdom. The bell, the kids, the laughing, and the talking—to Alec, all that seemed like sounds coming from some TV show in another room.

But a loud voice suddenly demanded his attention.

"Hey, can you guys *smell* something?"

Without looking up from his book, Alec knew the voice. It belonged to Kent Blair, a kid who lived on his street, a kid who used to be a friend. These days, Kent was very popular and very annoying, and he always laughed when Alec got in trouble. Kent was also in Alec's first-period art class, so him showing up like this? It wasn't a coincidence.

Alec forced his eyes to stay on the page, but he could tell Kent was about five feet away, standing with two other guys. He was talking extra loudly, making a big show of sniffing the air.

"*Phew!* Seriously, can't you *smell* that?"

One of the other guys said, "I think it's the spaghetti. From the cafeteria."

Kent turned slowly toward Alec and then pretended to see him for the first time. "Ohhh! *Look!*" He pointed. "That's Alec Spencer on the Hot Seat! So the smell? It's *fried bookworm*! Get it? Ha-ha!"

The other guys joined right in. "Oh—yeah! *Fried bookworm!*"

Alec looked up from his book and scowled. He was about to toss out some insults of his own, when all three guys stopped laughing and walked away—fast.

Something on his left moved, and Alec turned. It was Mrs. Vance, holding her office door open.

"You may come in now, Alec."

CHAPTER 2

Gulp

The chair in front of Mrs. Vance's desk was identical to the Hot Seat out in the hallway: hard red plastic with black metal legs. Alec remembered how big the chair had seemed back in first grade, and how scared he had been on those early visits. Today, the chair was a perfect fit, and he felt right at home.

Mrs. Vance looked the same: brownish-gray hair almost to her shoulders, a jacket over a blouse—sometimes it was a sweater over a blouse. And she always wore a necklace of small pearls. She didn't have what Alec would call a pretty face, but she wasn't anywhere near ugly either.

She was doing that thing where she rested her elbows on her desk and pressed the palms of both hands together. He thought it made her look like she was praying—maybe she was. Her glasses didn't have rims, and the lenses were sort of thick, so her brown eyes seemed larger than life. When she looked at him the way she was doing right then, Alec felt like a bug under a magnifying glass.

He knew better than to smile, and he knew better than to talk first. So he waited.

The wait was only five or ten seconds, but it felt much longer. Then Mrs. Vance pulled her hands apart and folded them in front of her on the desk. She spoke slowly and very softly, lips barely moving, her eyes narrowed.

"Alec, Alec, Alec—*what* are we going to do?" And as she said the word *do,* her dark eyebrows shot upward.

Alec sat perfectly still. Mrs. Vance had yelled at him before, she had shaken a finger in his face, and once she had slammed both hands down on her desk, hard. But this? *This* was new.

She opened a file folder on her desk. "I reviewed your academic results and test scores from last year. They weren't great, but they weren't as bad as I thought they might be." She paused and locked her large eyes onto his. "But in terms of your attitude reports, your study skills reports, and your class participation marks? Fifth grade was a disaster!" She paused, then asked, "Do you know how many times you were sent to my office last year for reading instead of listening and participating in class?"

Alec was about to guess eleven—but then decided he'd better keep his mouth shut. He shook his head.

Mrs. Vance leaned forward. "*Fourteen* times!"

Another long pause. "Your teachers and I know how bright you are, Alec. All of us admire how much you love to read—I don't think I have ever known anyone who enjoys books more than you do. But when reading gets in the way of your other schoolwork every single day? *That* is a problem, and it's gotten worse every year. Starting *today*, you have to make some definite changes—and you already know what they are. And if you choose *not* to change your classroom behavior? Then I will require that you attend a special study skills program. This program begins one week after school lets out next June, and the class meets for three hours each morning. The program lasts for six weeks, and unless your attitude and your actions change, *that* is how you will be spending most of next summer. Do you understand?"

Alec gulped, his mind spinning. A whole summer with no trip to New Hampshire, no time at his grandparents' cabin, no swimming in the lake—and no water-skiing!

The principal repeated her question. *"Do you understand?"*

"Yes."

"Good. I have told all your teachers to watch you closely, and if they see you reading in class or not paying attention, they are to send you directly to me. I'm also sending a registered letter to your parents, explaining how serious this has become. And after we see your behavior report and your grades for the first term, we'll take any further steps that are needed."

She filled out a yellow hall pass, ripped it from the pad, and slid it across the desk.

"Now get to your second-period class, and I don't want to see you in here again all year long."

Alec stood up, took the pass, and left her office without a word.

Autopilot

Six weeks of *summer school*? To learn study skills? It was a terrible thing to hear from the principal on the first day of sixth grade. But . . . as much as Alec hated that idea, Mrs. Vance had also said that he was smart and that he already knew what changes he had to make. It seemed pretty simple, really: All he had to do was stop reading during his classes and pay more attention.

So as Alec walked away from Mrs. Vance's office, he felt a little less worried with each step he took. Then he thought, *Did she really tell my teachers to keep a special lookout for me . . . or is that just something she says to all the kids who get in trouble?*

It was a fair question, and he got his answer quickly. Because when he arrived late for his second-period math class, Alec discovered that Mrs. Seward had saved him a seat in the very front row, smack in the center.

And when he got to Mr. Brock's third-period language arts class, again there was a front-row seat with his name on it. Alec was impressed with the principal's power to reach out and make him sit wherever she wanted him to.

However, this seating plan wasn't completely the principal's doing. Long before Mrs. Vance had spoken with them, his new teachers had already decided that Alec Spencer was going to sit front and center in each class—every single day of his sixth-grade life. And there was a reason for that.

Behind the closed door of the teachers' workroom, Alec was famous. At least once a week for the past four years, one of his teachers had blurted out something like, "You know how that Alec Spencer always has his nose in a book? The kid is an amazing reader, but it drives me *crazy*!" And two years earlier, Mrs. Vance had added a special notice to the *Parent and Student Handbook*—and all the teachers called this paragraph the Alec Rule:

READING LIBRARY BOOKS OR OTHER LITERATURE
DURING CLASS TIME IS ALLOWED ONLY WHEN A
TEACHER GIVES PERMISSION. EVERY STUDENT IS
EXPECTED TO PAY CAREFUL ATTENTION AND FULLY
PARTICIPATE IN ALL CLASSROOM ACTIVITIES.

However, the Alec Rule had been a total flop. It had failed to change the behavior of the one kid it had been written for.

But on this particular first day of school, the front-row treatment was working for Alec—especially after what Mrs. Vance had said to him at their meeting. He did not want to spend next summer stuck in a classroom, and from second period on, he didn't even *think* about trying to read during class.

In math, Mrs. Seward had given a speech about "the Future"—about how mathematics was the foundation for so many different careers. Alec had listened to every word she said.

During language arts, Mr. Brock had talked about the different kinds of essays they would have to write during middle school and high school, and how every student needed to get ready for all the hard work to come. And again Alec paid close attention, and he took careful notes about how to organize a five-paragraph essay. Sitting up front actually helped.

Then in fourth-period science, Mrs. Lowden started out with a slide-show speech that was a lot like the one in math class, except this talk was about how physics and chemistry and biology were going to be the keys to all the best careers in "the Future." The room was darkened so everyone could see the screen, and about two minutes into her talk, Alec switched off his ears and started thinking about *The High King*, about how the whole Chronicles of Prydain led up to this book . . . and how Taran had become a true warrior . . . and what it would feel like to swing a real sword, and how each battle was . . .

"Alec—don't you agree?"

Mrs. Lowden was staring into his face.

Alec blinked and said, "Oh—yeah . . . sure, I agree."

She said, "Good. Because I'd like *you* to be the one who keeps the list of the key concepts we'll need to review before our state tests in March and April. I'll make some space on a bulletin board for you."

There was a flutter of laughter from the class, which Mrs. Lowden silenced with one look. Alec sat up straight. He felt his face get warm, and he promised himself that he wouldn't daydream again. Tracking the key concepts in science class was going to be a miserable job . . . but Mrs. Lowden could have just yanked him out of his seat and sent him to Mrs. Vance. Which would have been worse— *much* worse.

The textbooks seemed thicker than ever, and class by class, Alec's book bag got heavier. This was the first year he had to change classes, and dashing to a different room every fifty-seven minutes made him feel like he was running a relay race. And, of course, each academic teacher assigned homework.

Alec had been looking forward to lunch—there was always some time to read in the cafeteria or out on the playground. Not today. The food lines seemed longer and slower, and he barely had time to gobble a plate of spaghetti and guzzle some milk before the bell rang. Then he had to check his schedule and rush to the far end of the building for social studies—he'd heard that Mrs. Henley was super strict about tardiness.

Changing classes made everything seem new today, and even though he felt stressed, the newness was also kind of exciting. But by the time he got back to his homeroom at the end of the day, all the excitement had drained away. Alec felt frazzled and dazed, and he knew what he needed. He needed to dive into a story and stay there, all alone inside a great book.

When the last bell rang at 2:53, he was off at a gallop. Operating on full autopilot, Alec heaved his book bag onto one shoulder and lurched along through the halls and out the front doors, all the way to his regular spot in the bus lines.

He sat down right there on the sidewalk, opened up *The High King,* and began to read. But after just a few sentences, Alec felt a sharp jab on his shoulder. Startled, he looked up, half blinded by the afternoon sun. It was his little brother, Luke.

"Get lost!" Alec snapped, and turned back to his book.

Luke poked him again with the corner of his iPad. "Where are you supposed to be right now?"

"*Duh,*" Alec said, "waiting for the bus—and here it comes."

"No," Luke said. "Think again."

Alec stared straight ahead a moment, then said, "Oh . . . *ohh!* Right! I forgot!"

He jumped to his feet, grabbed his bag, and followed Luke back into the school. Luke was trotting, so Alec had to walk fast to keep up.

Now he remembered the conversation at dinner one night a couple of weeks ago—except he had been eating and reading and listening all at the same time . . . but mostly reading. It was a Wimpy Kid book, so he'd been laughing, too.

Still, he recalled his mom and dad explaining that they were each starting new jobs in September—jobs at two different companies near Boston. Which meant they would both have to drive to work every day.

His parents were computer programmers, and for the past eleven years they had worked from home. So this was a big change. And since neither of them would get home from work until almost dinnertime, Alec and Luke had been enrolled in the Extended Day Program—three extra hours at school every afternoon.

Hurrying along behind his brother, Alec felt kind of pleased with himself. Because even though the craziness of this first day had made him forget, and even though he didn't have all the details clear in his mind, he *had* captured most of the important ideas—which was sort of the way it felt when he took math tests . . . and science and language arts and social studies tests. Except *that* was going to have to change—and when the letter from Mrs. Vance arrived at home? There would be fireworks . . . the bad kind.

When they got to where the two main corridors crossed, Luke stopped.

Alec said, "How come you came looking for me at the bus stop?"

"Because after dinner last night, Mom told me I had to check up on you."

"Oh."

Luke pointed. "You go to the gym. I'll be in the cafeteria."

"What? How come?"

"Because of the directions in the booklet they sent us," Luke said. "Kindergarten through third-grade kids report to the cafeteria, and fourth, fifth, and sixth graders report to the gym. Did you pack a snack this morning?"

Alec's face was blank. "Snack?"

"Yes, 'snack'—that's what humans call food they eat in between their main meals."

For a nerdy third grader, Luke was getting pretty good at sarcasm. Alec smiled. "No—no snack."

Luke reached into his backpack and handed Alec a granola bar and a box of apple juice.

Alec made a face. "You don't have chips, or Cheetos, or something . . . good?"

Luke ignored him. He flipped back the cover of his iPad and looked at the time. "You're four minutes late. If you don't check in by seven minutes after three, they call the school office and the parents, and if you're more than fifteen minutes late, they alert the police. Mom's picking us up outside the gym at six." Then he turned and trotted toward the cafeteria.

Alec marched straight ahead. The door of the gym was only about a minute away, and during that short walk he realized something.

When this idea had first come up back in August, he had been sure that three extra hours at school had to be the *worst* possible way to end each day. But if sixth grade was really going to be the way today had just been? That changed everything.

Suddenly, those same three hours every afternoon felt like a gift from the friendly universe—his own personal chunk of time, with no one to bother him and nothing to do but read and read and read.

There was no doubt in Alec's mind: The Extended Day Program had just become the best part of his whole sixth-grade year.

CHAPTER 4

Rules

Alec got to the gym at exactly six minutes after three. He checked in at the table by the door, then walked halfway down the west wall of the huge room, flopped onto a pile of exercise mats beside the bleachers, and opened up *The High King*—again.

Almost twenty minutes later, a voice interrupted the story—again.

"Excuse me, you're Alec, right?"

He sat up quickly. "Yes . . . Alec Spencer."

It was the woman who had taken his name at the door, looking down at him through narrow glasses with brown plastic frames. She had short blond hair and small gold earrings shaped like cats. A dangly bracelet hung from the wrist of the same hand that had rings on it, and Alec couldn't help noticing that her fingers were long and thin, finished off with bright red nail polish—which immediately made him remember the warden in the book *Holes*, the lady who ran a boys' prison camp out in the desert.

She said, "Did you get the student information booklet about Extended Day, about your program choices?"

"Yes," he said, "it's at home . . . except I didn't get a chance to look at it."

The woman said, "I see. Well, I'm Mrs. Case, the program director, and you have three different options: You can sign up for the Active Games Program or the Clubs Program, or you can report to the Homework Room each afternoon."

Mrs. Case tried to smile as she talked to him, but Alec could tell she was annoyed that he hadn't known all this beforehand.

"So, those are your choices," she said.

Alec said, "But . . . can't I just sit here and read?"

Mrs. Case shook her head. "You need to be enrolled in one of the three activities I mentioned—clubs, games, or homework. Now, if that book is a school assignment, then you should be in room 407, the Homework Room."

Alec said, "This book? It's just for fun—and I've already read it four times!" He smiled, but Mrs. Case didn't smile back.

She looked over the top of her glasses at him. "But you do *have* homework, don't you?"

He nodded. "Oh, yeah—tons!"

"So you *could* go to the Homework Room and work on that."

"Well," he said slowly, "I *could,* but I'm going to do all that later, at home . . . because it's *homework*—get it?"

Alec was still smiling, and Mrs. Case still wasn't.

"As it also explains in your information booklet, students have these first two days to decide which of the three activities to start out with. If you don't want to be in the Homework Room, you could ask Mr. Jenson or his assistants about Active Games. Or you could talk to Mr. Willner—he's in charge of the Clubs Program, and he can tell you all about that."

Mrs. Case looked at Alec for a moment and then gave him a real smile. "The games can be a lot of fun—and if you don't see a club you like, you could always start one of your own. Extended Day is actually a great place to spend time with kids you might never get to know during the regular school year. But whatever you choose to do, you can't just lie down over here on the gym mats by yourself, all right? So, have a nice afternoon, and if you have any other questions, I'll be happy to answer them."

And with that, Mrs. Case turned and walked back toward her command center at the main door of the gym. She was wearing a dark blue pants suit, which made her look sort of like a police officer. Except she also wore orange-and-white running shoes, which was *not* like a police officer. Alec noticed the shoes because they squeaked on the shiny wood floor.

The big clock above the main door was inside a heavy wire cage to protect it from stray basketballs, and he could see that it was almost three-thirty. In the corner off to the right of the doorway, it looked like a game of kickball was starting up, but Alec didn't want to play active games for the next two and a half hours—he'd gotten plenty of exercise hurrying from class to class all day. So he tucked his book into his backpack and headed toward the clubs area.

Five cafeteria tables had been set up along the rear wall, each about fifteen feet from the next, and a tall man wearing a blue sweater was helping some kids unload plastic bins from a storage closet in the corner. There was a small hand-lettered sign on each table: CHESS CLUB, ROBOTICS CLUB, CHINESE CLUB, LEGO CLUB, and ORIGAMI CLUB.

Alec didn't really want to be in a club either . . . and he *really* didn't want to start one. To have to get an activity organized and then keep it going, day after day? That sounded horrible. Because right now, today? All he wanted to do was read.

Alec glanced back to see if Mrs. Case was watching him. She wasn't, so he hurried toward the table with the most kids, which was the Lego Club—three boys and three girls. The tallest boy was lifting trays of Lego parts out of a large bin and handing them to the other kids. Alec didn't know any of them—he was pretty sure they were all fifth graders.

When he reached the table, he smiled at everyone, and said, "Mind if I sit here and read? I won't bother anybody."

The tall boy shrugged and said, "No problem," and most of the other kids nodded.

Then one of the girls said, "But if you want to join the club, you have to get on Mr. Willner's list."

"Right. I'll remember that."

Alec glanced across the gym once more to check on Mrs. Case . . . all clear. He quickly moved around to the back side of the table, slid onto the seat across from the big plastic bin, and hunched down behind it, nicely hidden. Then he took out *The High King* and started to read once more.

The story lifted him up and carried him away, just like it always did, and he forgot all about the *squeak, squeak, squeak* of Mrs. Case's running shoes. Even though he knew this book as well as he knew his own backyard, he still loved every character, still loved every twist and turn of the plot. And after a day like this one, it felt amazingly wonderful to know *exactly* what was going to happen next.

About the Author

George Clements

ANDREW CLEMENTS is the *New York Times* bestselling author of the beloved modern classic *Frindle,* which has sold over six million copies, won nineteen state awards (and been nominated for thirty-eight!), and been translated into over a dozen languages. Andrew began writing while he was a public school teacher outside of Chicago. He has watched many fads come and go, from the yo-yo to the fidget spinner, and even a paper palm tree fad that once swept his classroom (and was later described in a book). Called the "master of school stories" by *Kirkus Reviews,* Andrew is now the author of over eighty acclaimed books for kids, including, most recently, *The Losers Club,* which *School Library Journal* called "engaging and funny . . . a laugh-out-loud first purchase" in a starred review. Andrew lives in Maine with his wife, Becky. They have four grown sons and two rascally cats.

AndrewClements.com